Five Reflections

Five Reflections

Sara E. Spivey

VANTAGE PRESS
New York

Cover design by Susan Thomas

FIRST EDITION

All rights reserved, including the right of
reproduction in whole or in part in any form.

Copyright © 2003 by Sara E. Spivey

Published by Vantage Press, Inc.
516 West 34th Street, New York, New York 10001

Manufactured in the United States of America
ISBN: 0-533-14534-1

Library of Congress Catalog Card No.: 2003090493

0 9 8 7 6 5 4 3 2 1

To my mother, Ruth,
and my daughters, Amanda and Katie

Five Reflections

It is cold and dreary now. This iron-gray solitude used to be her companion, the desolateness of this place in winter, a lasting friend. Only the reflections of the sky, the sand, and the water held her attention for any length of time. This place created a presence for her, a place that was buried deep inside—a presence that lasted long past the time when the short days of winter stretched themselves into spring and lazy summer haze. I could always see it. But it has been gone for some time, and I know I must be patient for the next. It will come.

Of this, I am certain.

Beth—2002

It was unusual for fog this time of year. Usually the winter months brought cold, clear weather. Fog was reserved for the summer months, when all the tourists descended like a plague, surprised by northern beaches and their climates. The sweatshirt vendors always did a brisk business in July and August.

They sat huddled on the porch, and both of them were thinking independently that maybe this wasn't the right thing for them, but neither of them spoke. They waited silently for several minutes, awash in their own thoughts, until she broke the silence.

She glanced at her watch. "Three-thirty," she said. "Even if this fog does lift, we'll have seven minutes of sun before it rolls back in."

"I'm not overly optimistic about that scenario coming to fruition. I wouldn't plan on a sunset cocktail today." Drew stood up and began to walk up the path to the driveway, as if he could coax the arrival. He shoved his hands deeper into his pockets to try to warm them.

Beth glanced at her watch again.

"Where is this guy, anyway? He said to meet him here at three." Patience was not one of Beth's strong suits.

"The fog was pretty thick coming across the bridge. If there was an accident behind me, he could be tied up. You're not going back to the office are you?" Drew looked down at his watch and quickly calculated that even if the guy showed up in the next five minutes, getting back into the city before five wasn't likely.

"I wasn't planning on it, but I'd like to see this place in some semblance of daylight, and the sun sets so early."

Just then, a set of headlights cut through the fog and into the driveway. The car rolled slowly to the back of the house, and the driver turned off the ignition. When he got out of the car, Beth was surprised. *Not what I was picturing,* she thought. When he had told her he was the executor of the estate that owned the property, she was expecting old. This guy was tall, probably in his mid-fifties, and impeccably dressed. *So much for the low-ball offer*, she thought. This guy didn't seem like an easy mark.

He bounded up the path and onto the porch, where they had been waiting. Now that he was closer, Beth noticed that he probably was older than she initially thought, but very well cared for. He had an air about him. Money. That was it. He had a lot of money.

"My apologies for leaving you here on the porch. I left my office a few minutes late, and instead of making up the time, the fog just exacerbated my situation." He extended his hand to Drew. Beth looked at his hands and noticed they were very well manicured.

"I'm Robert Allen. We spoke on the phone. A pleasure to meet you, Drew. And this must be Beth." He turned to meet her gaze and extended his hand. Beth shook it quickly.

"Well, why don't I let you two have a look around?"

He fumbled in his jacket pocket for a moment and then brought out a single key. It was held by a key chain that had a monogram, but she couldn't quite make out the initials. It didn't look like the first letter was "R," but before she could see it, it was back in his pocket. He gently nudged the door open, before realizing it was being held back by a disorganized stack of mail. Beth noticed now that the mail slot was in the front door.

"She's been dead for four months. Still gets plenty of mail." He shook his head and then scooped up the loose mail in one arm, while pushing the door open the remainder of the way. "The views are lovely from the living room and of course the front deck. It's not very spacious, but as they say in the real estate game, 'location, location, location.'"

He smiled, and Beth thought to herself, *wonder how much all that location is worth?*

"Feel free to roam about. I'll just stay in the kitchen, out of the way. I have a few phone calls to make. If you have questions, feel free to interrupt me."

Beth and Drew began to look around the place. It was small, but that suited them just fine, since it would be the two of them and maybe an occasional guest.

They had decided when they got married that neither of them wanted children. They both wanted to work as hard as they could, make as much money as possible, and be able to retire at forty. That was the plan. It was hard to tell which one of them was more driven, but for people who knew them both, Beth probably got the nod. Whatever drove her came from a place deep inside, which no one really understood, even her husband.

She had been an overachiever practically from the womb. Phrases like "the youngest ever to" and "the highest of" always preceded her accomplishments. She had gone further and faster than any of her contemporaries at college or graduate school. She was in her fourth year at a prestigious management consulting firm, on track for partner in the next year, two years ahead of her cohorts. She told friends that she married Drew because they made a good "merged asset." She had carefully selected him and then went about the business of falling in love.

They had been talking about a place on this stretch of beach for four years. They had a nice home in the city, but they wanted a place out here for weekends, and if they executed their plans, they could live out here full time in another few years. Close enough to city life but far enough to feel as though they were away.

They walked from room to room, checking the views from each window. They both paused in the bathroom, looking out a ship's porthole in the space above the sink, where a mirror would have been in most homes.

"Well, this has to be a better view in the morning than the one I usually see," Drew quipped. "Tough for shaving, though."

"She lived alone. Nobody was shaving in the mirror." Beth gazed out the porthole and took in the view of the ocean. "I think it's inspired."

Because of the placement on the lot, at an angle, the ocean could be seen from almost every room, with the exception of the entry from the driveway, which was small and dark. The view from the front room and the deck beyond was spectacular. Although it was foggy, Beth seemed pretty certain that you could make out the bridge from here and, probably, the city behind it. The view to the north was jagged and mostly sheer cliff, and every now and then a glimpse of Highway 1 could be seen, a small car snaking along its curves. She thought it odd that this stretch of beach had so few homes. To both the north and south of this, the homes seemed much closer together.

"This stretch of beach seems so unpopulated. Why is that?" she asked Mr. Allen, who had the phone to his ear but didn't seem to be in conversation. He switched it off and looked up at her.

"In 1960, when Thea bought the house, there were only about four homes, all built in the 1950s. Sometime in the mid-fifties, probably after a particularly stormy winter, people got concerned about the erosion being caused by construction. For several years out here, 100 to 150 feet of beach was being lost each year. So, they clamped down on new construction. Various attempts have been made to relax the building restrictions, but the environmentalists are pretty entrenched up here, so it's never been done.

"There was a lot of concern that increased building would accelerate the erosion and so the county placed a moratorium on this three-quarter-mile strip. Nowhere else, though. It's probably because the beach is narrower in this strip. To the north and south, a good quarter-mile exists between the lot lines and the ocean. Here, it's less than five hundred feet, and although the walk to the water looks fairly level, it actually falls off at a pretty good pitch. You'll notice it when you walk down to the water. I guess that's what makes this property more rare."

Translation: expensive, Beth thought as he finished. The price was higher than the range they had set for themselves, but she was already putting together her case for Drew. The fact was that she was exhausted from looking and she loved this location. The house was old, and it would need more money dumped into it to suit her taste, particularly if they were going to entertain out here. But it was quite well laid out and though it had only 1,400 square feet, it felt larger.

The high ceiling and the glass windows in the front room opened the house up such that it felt larger. The living area actually felt like it brought the ocean in from the outside. And the sound of the waves was so relaxing. She was already imagining what it would be like to fall asleep to that sound. When the waves broke up close to the shoreline, the bubbling on the rocks as the water receded sounded like popcorn being popped in the next room. Just loud enough to be recognizable, quiet enough to be soothing.

Much of the house was the original equipment. It would definitely need some work in the kitchen and in the bathroom. Although it was well kept, it felt, well, old.

"I'm surprised that nothing has been updated," Beth said to Mr. Allen. "Most of the homes we've looked at up here have had a lot of renovating." Two could play at this game of "The Price is Right."

"I suspect many of the other homes you've seen have had a few more residents in them. Vacation homes tend to have pretty good turnover. People get tired of the location after a while, want to try another spot. Each new owner renovates another piece. But Thea had lived out here since 1960, used it as a writing studio as well as her home. She was a novelist. Dorothea Renton? She had an apartment in San Francisco, but she wrote out here, mostly in the winters when the beach was deserted." He paused a moment and looked around the kitchen, the dining area, and the main room beyond. "I suppose she never saw the need to change it. It suited her needs."

"Dorothea Renton as in *Still Life* Dorothea Renton?" Beth asked.

"Yes, among others. She was quite a prolific writer after she moved out here. I think she wrote about one a year for a stretch there."

"You seem to know a lot about her, but you're not related?"

He smiled.

"My mother and Thea were best friends, 'soulmates,' I think people call it now, for almost sixty years. I have wonderful memories of her, and of this place," he said, glancing around the empty rooms. "My mom would bring us here in the summer when Thea wasn't using it, and my mother spent a little time out here with her when she was writing."

The house was entirely empty with the exception of one item. On the southeast wall of the main room hung the ugliest mirror Beth had ever seen. *That will have to go. I'm sure there was a reason for it*, but with nothing else in the whole house, and being such an outdated style, it seemed drastically out of place. It was a strange color, sort of a coke-bottle green, and it looked like it had been "antiqued," probably in the sixties, when that was popular. Some of the color was peeling off, and it was hanging slightly askew. But she did notice that the placement of the mirror provided quite a nice view of the beach to the north. *Well, I suppose that's why it was put there*, Beth thought.

"What's with the mirror?" Beth asked.

"Oh, yes, the mirror. That's something you'll need to know about. Thea's will expressly stipulates that the mirror is not to be moved from that location."

Beth and Drew looked at each other, trading looks of

dismay. This was an interesting twist.

"You're kidding, right? We can't move the mirror?" Beth wanted to make absolutely certain she had heard him correctly.

He glanced down at the floor, seemingly embarrassed by the request, as though he realized they might think he was making it up just to see their reaction.

"I'm afraid not. The contract terms for the sale of the house will be quite particular about that term." He stared at the mirror and said softly, "I imagine it must have quite a history." He paused briefly, and then added, "However, the will doesn't say anything about painting or refinishing it, so the buyer is free to do that if he so chooses. You know, to blend with your taste." He thought this might soften the blow a bit, make it a little more palatable. He looked at their faces and could see it didn't seem to appease them much.

"I have never heard of anything so strange. How do you plan to enforce it? Once the house is sold, you can't exactly be pulling sneak inspections."

Beth's tone was slightly raw, and she realized she had probably just sealed their fate. If the mirror was that important, this guy wasn't selling to anyone that he thought wouldn't uphold the request.

She quickly tried to recover.

"I mean, I personally like it, but you know, not everyone will." She smiled sweetly, hoping she had gotten herself out of the hole she'd just dug.

Drew looked over at her as if to say, "Nicely done, dear. Now that you've blown this deal, what next?"

"I believe the idea is to sell the home to someone who likes the mirror and won't be troubled by its staying there. If it's an issue for you, then I assume you won't be interested in the house." His tone had turned slightly terse, and Beth noticed the vein in his temple was pulsing.

"It's not an issue," Beth offered, a bit too quickly. Still trying to dig herself out of the enormous hole she had found herself in, she decided to take a new tack. "And you don't know anything about it or why it's to stay. Its history, maybe?"

"I'm sorry, I don't. It's been in that spot for as long as I can remember coming here, but I don't know much more than that."

The sun was lowering in the sky, and miraculously, the fog had actually lifted just enough to see that it was going to be a spectacular sunset. The fog was still hanging in over the water, but the tiniest of slivers had opened on the horizon, just so the sun could peek through. It was as if the sun needed to make a grand exit and, like Moses parting the Red Sea, it had forced an opening. Beth wanted to stay long enough to see it so she would be able to get a sense of the place in a different light. She also assumed they'd be spending time watching it set from the deck when they were out here. Because Stinson was a southern-facing beach, the sun didn't just drop off the edge of the ocean out here, but rather eked away over the cliffs just to the north.

"Do you mind if we stay a few more minutes to watch the sun go down?" Beth asked. "And I'd like to take a few pictures of the place if that's okay."

"Feel free. The light out here is a very important part of how the place will feel to you. The sunset can be quite dramatic." Beth noticed that he looked at his own reflection in the mirror as he finished his sentence.

"How many parties do you have interested in the

house?" Drew inquired.

"We've shown it to several folks, but it's not ideal for everybody. It's small, so it's not great for a family. And, as you pointed out, it will need some updating for a more social lifestyle. As I said earlier, Thea used it as a writing studio mostly. I'm not sure she ever had guests out here."

Beth came back from retrieving her camera in the car. She had been thinking more about the mirror.

"Is your mother still living?" she inquired. From her tone, it was clear to Mr. Allen that she wasn't asking just to make conversation. Even though he had met her only thirty minutes ago, Mr. Allen knew that she had an agenda.

"Yes, she is still living, but she has Alzheimer's disease. Some days, she's pretty lucid, other days, completely incoherent."

"Do you think she could tell me anything about that mirror?"

"It's possible, although I wouldn't count on it. When she talks about her past, some parts are quite clear, but then she mixes things up with the present. It's hard to tell the line between fact and fiction on some days."

Beth took a few photos of the kitchen and the master bedroom and then proceeded to the front room. She became absolutely motionless when she walked into the living room. What she saw left her breathless. The sun had just fallen behind the cliffs, and the opening in the fog left just enough space to create light on the cloudy sky, which turned the lingering fog into a brilliant palette of color. At the base of the opening, a brilliant ruby red faded back to a lighter pink, then into a pale orange, and then a rosish blue.

The colors and the light from the sky completely

filled the room. It was as if the entire room had been painted in the sunset and the room felt as if the sun was setting right inside. Beth slowly turned in the room, taking it all in when at last her eyes met the mirror. It was entirely filled with the horizon and was bathing the reflection onto her. Perhaps it was the shape of the mirror or the position in which it was hanging or the way the light hung in it, but the mirror actually brought the sunset into the house. Long after the color vanished from the sky, the pale palette of blue, lavender, and pink stayed in the room.

Drew, having stayed in the kitchen to chat with Mr. Allen, trying to discern what it would take to get the place, walked into the room behind her a moment later.

"Have I missed—"

He stopped midsentence as he stared at her reflection in the mirror and saw the color wash over her face. In five years of marriage, he wasn't sure he had ever really seen her face until this moment. They both turned slowly to take in the entire landscape of the room and the effect the light had on the mirror and simply stared in wonder.

"The mirror stays," Beth whispered.

"The mirror stays," he replied.

Robert Allen stood in the kitchen and silently smiled. *The mirror stays*, he thought.

"So, how was the house? Is it perfect?"

Kim Baxter had been Beth's assistant since she started at the firm. She had gone through the trials and tribulations of at least fifty other "perfect" houses, none of which had come to fruition. So she asked somewhat facetiously, knowing what the answer would be, but hoping for better.

Beth scratched her head.

"It's as close to perfect as we are going to get, I think. We're putting an offer in tonight, but I'm not getting my hopes up. We have been here before, as you well know. There is at least one other bidder, and I'm sure we're going to have to go over the asking price. We just haven't settled on how much over yet."

"Dan and Bill want to see you as soon as you're ready. They seem a little edgy. You wouldn't know anything about that would you?"

"Of course, they're edgy. It's Monday. Always edgy on Mondays." Beth rolled her eyes, grabbed her coffee and headed down the hall. "Whose office?"

"Dan's," Kim replied. "Always Dan's for bad news, Bill's for good. Your rule, remember?" Kim never took her eyes off her computer screen as she said this.

Beth nodded, although she was hoping the pattern wasn't the same this morning. She wasn't in the mood for a confrontation with these two. In her four years at the firm, she'd had several run-ins with the partners, mostly differences of opinions on recommendations for clients. She'd spend three or four months working on an assignment, put together the "get well" plan, and most of the time Dan and Bill came to the same conclusions.

On one or two occasions, they differed. Beth hated to be wrong. She also hated to be overruled by either of them. But, as Drew reminded her, until the name on the front door was Breyer, McSwain and Graham, as opposed to just Breyer, McSwain and Associates, Bill and Dan got to have the last word. Rank had privilege. A lesson that was tough for Beth to swallow, but swallow it she did. So as she headed down the hall, she was preparing herself for some sort of crow-eating. She just didn't know what kind exactly.

She could tell she was in the wringer for something by Dan's posture. He always sat incredibly erect when he was pissed off.

"Kim said you wanted to see me?"

As she opened the door she saw Bill as well, seated near the window. This was his usual position for a scolding, staring out the window in a somewhat contemplative posture, as though he was thinking about what he was going to say. In reality, he knew exactly what he was going to say, but over the years, he had convinced himself that if he looked like he was making it up as he went along, the person getting browbeaten didn't feel so badly.

Beth went on the offensive immediately. "You both have that tsk, tsk, tsk look of a disappointed father. Does one of you want to tell me why that is?"

"You sent Spencer Morrison to Minneapolis to do management interviews last week?" Bill asked, without breaking his gaze out the window.

"Yes, I did. He was ready."

"We decide when he is ready," Dan shot back, looking her squarely in the eye.

"You asked me to run this engagement. My understanding is that includes the running of the people on the engagement as well. I needed Claire here with me to finish the competitive research, and so I sent Spencer."

"He's a research associate, for Christ's sake. He's been out of college for two years. He can't interview senior management solo. What the hell were you thinking?"

Dan was pretty hot now; the veins in his neck were

pulsing. In the four years that she had worked for him, this just might have been the tightest squeeze she'd been in. But she stuck to her guns and didn't waiver. If she had learned one thing about Dan in the four years she had been here, it was that he couldn't stand weak character. Anyone who caved under fire was deemed to lack the resolve required for this job, and it didn't take long before they were "counseled out." She'd seen a lot of good, young talent shown the door, and she was determined she wouldn't be one of them.

"Look, Spencer is young, I agree. But he knows the work to be done here, and he's ready to take on more. He's not uncomfortable doing interviews. Besides, he wasn't winging it; we worked on the guide together. When he went last week, he was ready."

"Well, the CEO called me this morning and is hotter than a ten-acre pepper patch. Says he doesn't appreciate us sending in 'moles' to question his employees. Said he thought we were trying to help him, not hinder him."

"And I'm sure you were quick to explain that in order to help him save his job, we're going to have to ask some uncomfortable questions about the decisions he makes. He may not like the answers that his managers give us," Beth fired back. "You did tell him that, right?"

She was growing impatient, but she knew she had to keep it together. "Look, Dan, you and I both know this has nothing to do with Spencer Morrison talking to people. This is all about what those people are telling him, and somebody wanting to cover that up."

Dan sighed, and Bill finally broke his gaze from the glass.

"Beth, this is an important client for us. Almost two

million dollars last year in billing. We can't afford to piss him off."

"Dan, he would have been pissed off if you had been doing the interviewing personally. This has nothing to do with my sending Spencer. He's using it as an excuse. He's paranoid about the possibility of us uncovering a whole string of management fuck-ups that he willingly supported because he got lazy. Don't hang Spencer out to dry for that. Or me either, for that matter."

Dan and Bill looked at each other and then both looked at Beth.

She looked back at Dan and figured she should just go for the brass ring.

"Dan, how long have you known he was in way over his head?"

"I've known him for twenty years. 'Over his head' doesn't begin to cover it."

He almost looked like he was stifling a smile, but that might have been Beth's optimistic imagination. She leaned on the back of the chair.

"Look, I can back off this if you want me to, although personally, I think, for the shareholders, that would be irresponsible."

"The shareholders aren't paying us," Bill said.

"No, they're not. But we are supposed to be providing an independent and unbiased review here, which ultimately leads to long-term success for the company. That is the objective, right? I'm not confused about that, am I?"

Now Dan gazed out the window and said nothing for what seemed an agonizingly long period of time.

"No, keep going. I'll talk to him, let him know what's evolving and see what he wants to do."

"Okay. But that probably means the three of us are going to have more of these conversations. If every time I ask a question he doesn't like, he's calling you to complain, we're not going to get much done."

Now it was Bill's turn.

"All we're asking is that you turn up your sensitivity a little, that's all. It's highly likely that when you finish this job, this guy is going to be looking for one. Just try to put the baseball bat away when you're with him, okay?"

Beth took a deep breath.

"Message received. Will comply."

She turned on her heels and walked back to her office. This was always her downfall. She was aggressive, hard-nosed; "caustic" had been used to describe her on more than one occasion. She just couldn't figure out the balance between passion and compassion when it came to her work. Every manager she had ever worked with gave her the same feedback. Smart, talented, insensitive. If she wanted to make partner next year, she would have to turn this around, and she knew it. Being good at the work wasn't enough. She had to force herself to be good at managing the relationships too.

"Well, that was fun," she said to Kim as she walked by her cubicle. "Remind me to stop making any and all decisions without a permission slip." She walked into her office and slammed the door behind her.

After a few minutes, Kim thought it was probably safe to enter.

"I guess they weren't so keen on you sending Spencer, huh?"

She gazed out her window and watched a container ship coming into the bay; heading for Oakland, she assumed. *What would it be like to be on that thing for two months*, she thought.

She looked back at Kim.

"Doesn't really have anything to do with Spencer. He just provided the excuse. Dan's friend isn't going to look so good here, and he's worried."

"Did he tell you to back off?"

"No. He told me to be more sensitive to his situation," she said, emphasizing the word sensitive in a somewhat sarcastic tone.

Kim laughed out loud.

"Oh, that's rich. I don't think your name and the word sensitive have been uttered in the same sentence since the day you were born."

"Yeah, that's pretty much what I told him," said Beth, smiling back at Kim. "You remember that mailer we got for 'sensitivity training' from the AMA? Did you save that? I might need that."

They both giggled.

"As I recall," Kim said, "you said that stuff was for touchy-feely weaklings, as you threw it into the trash."

"I did not do that." Beth paused and then added, "It sounds like something I'd do, though." They both laughed. Kim knew her weaknesses better than anyone but didn't seem to be able to help her with them either.

"Hey, not to change the subject, but let's," Beth said, brightening a little. "I have a little project for you this morning. Find me a furniture guy, some sort of appraiser or something. I'm not sure whom I need. If we get this house, there is this one little weird stipulation."

"What's that?"

"There is a god-awful mirror that is not to be moved

from its present location. It's got some hideous kind of antique green paint on it, and I just want to find out what's underneath, how old it is, you know, to see if I can figure out a way to live with it in that spot. Maybe we can give it a makeover. Get it on *Oprah*."

"You can't move it?"

"Not according to the executor of the estate. I'm not sure they'd ever check, but I'd hate to go against a dead person's dying wish and then end up with weird ghost noises in the house." She paused momentarily and added, "It just seems like it has a story to tell, and I thought I might find someone who can help me figure out what it is."

"Okay, I'll see what I can find. How late are you staying today?"

"Late. I have to practice being sensitive, remember? Is there no end to what I will do for my brilliant career?"

"Do I note a hint of sarcasm?" Kim replied as she turned towards the door.

"Oh, no, not me." Beth turned back to the window and watched the same container ship slowly crawling through the bay, making its way east. She picked up the phone and dialed Drew's office. Expecting to get his voice mail, she was surprised when she heard his voice.

"Oh, hi. I didn't expect you to pick up. I'm just calling to remind you that we have to be there at six tonight to present this offer. You will be there, right? You're not going to forget, run late, blow this off? I know you're not as keen on this place as I am, so it would be like you to come up with some lame excuse—"

"This is the third time you have reminded me since six forty-five this morning. I'll be there Beth; 333 California, Robert Allen's office. I've got it. Not to worry. And I am 'keen,' to use your word. I think it will be a great place to take my girlfriend."

"You are a pig."

"Yes, but a pig with money to spend on a second home, which makes me worth putting up with. Hey, I've got to start thinking about my trophy wife now, or all the good ones will be gone."

"That's droll. Did you talk to anyone about this weird clause, about the mirror?" Beth was still hoping there might be an out.

"Well, two out of the three real estate partners here agreed that it's probably not enforceable, but to remove it would break the spirit of the agreement, written by a dead person, I might quickly add, and we'd be cursed forever. Besides, I thought we decided that it stayed?"

"We did. What did the third one say?"

"He said we should find another property. He was pretty certain the first night we were there, a whole band of gypsies would arrive to channel with their medium."

Beth laughed. Of all the qualities Drew possessed, his sense of humor was definitely at the top of the list—he interrupted her thoughts.

"Did you find any furniture gurus that can take a look at it? Maybe suggest a good twelve-step rehab program?"

"Gee, between getting Dan and Bill off the ledge this morning without actually getting out there with them, I've been a little busy. I kind of thought my day job ought to take precedence, being a Monday and all. Would be a shame to get sacked while we are trying to get approved for a loan."

"Sorry." He didn't sound sorry. He sounded preoccupied. She could hear paper-shuffling noises in the background.

"However, I did have Kim make a few phone calls. I'll let you know what she found out when I see you at five forty-five."

"That's my girl. I thought you said six?"

"Five forty-five is Drew time for six."

"Are you handling me?"

"It's a full-time job, baby." She was hanging up the phone as Kim walked into her office.

"Okay, I found three guys who'll take a look. All antique dealers, so if it's a cheesy piece of plywood that was glued together in 1965, you'll have spent $125 for nothing. Here are the names and numbers. I would suggest that you actually own the mirror before you have someone tinkering with it, but that's just me."

Kim had a knack for sarcasm that Beth normally appreciated, but this afternoon it was getting on her nerves.

"Thanks for the names. You can keep the editorial."

The list was an eclectic mix. One guy in Mill Valley (close to Stinson; maybe his fee would be lower), one guy on Maiden Lane, and one guy down in the Mission District. The last one seemed odd. The Mission District wasn't exactly a hotbed for antique furniture. They'd know tonight if they had the house, so Beth made a note on her calendar to call one in the morning, assuming she still needed their services.

Beth's curiosity was piqued. But she already knew that even if a furniture dealer could tell her the origin of the piece, it was unlikely that he could tell her its history. That was going to require a more thoughtful plan.

Is there any more contented look than that of young, unbridled, enthusiasm? The glistening of the eyes, the glow and fullness of the face with the anticipation of all that is to come. The reflection is lovely in just the right light: at the dimming of the day or just at sunrise when the light is soft and the silhouette is the only thing that can be seen with any clarity. From this view, I can see that he is apprehensive, but not afraid. His hazy view of the unknown is clearer to me, but then that is the beauty of seeing the actual image rather than the reflection. It is not up to me to wrestle with the emotion that underlies the reflection.

That is his struggle.

Thomas—1881

He had been taken on as an apprentice over three years ago, and he had learned the craft well. He considered it an incredible stroke of good fortune that Mr. Morris had asked him on. He took on only a dozen new apprentices each year, and Thomas's credentials were not exactly top-notch. But Mr. Morris saw talent in his work, an intricacy in detail that was made obvious by his careful selection of wood and pattern. William Morris was sure he could make him into a fine craftsman. He had good skills, but more importantly, he had vision and imagination. He also had passion, and that was what distinguished him from the others.

In the years that Thomas was apprenticed to William Morris, he worked on several commissions for prominent London families, and Mr. Morris had taken on several commissions for the royal family as well. There was a rumor in the shop that another commission had arrived from the queen, so it was with great excitement and also some anxiety that he went to Mr. Morris's office when summoned.

"Ah, Thomas, come in. I have something I wish to speak with you about." William Morris had a deep, booming voice that resonated in the room long after he had stopped speaking. In fact, when he spoke at an accelerated pace, it often required great concentration to follow him and not get lost in the echo from earlier words.

"Yes, sir. You wanted to see me, sir?" Thomas inquired a bit anxiously.

"I've summoned you in response to a request I have received for a commission. It strikes me that you might be the right person to assist me with the job. It will require careful consideration, and I believe you can be of great help to me."

Thomas had worked on several commissions in the last six months as Mr. Morris's assistant, but he sensed this to be different. On those pieces, Mr. Morris began the design and then asked Thomas to assist him as the work progressed. To be asked to assist in the design was a great honor, and was normally reserved for the more experienced craftsmen. Thomas was pleased but also a bit perplexed as to why it was he who was chosen.

"The commissioner would like a dressing mirror. The wood is to be cherry. All other aspects of the design can be ours, within reason. The piece should conform to reasonable Victorian design. The choice of cherry wood is quite unusual, really, considering that all the other pieces have been in walnut or mahogany. Work on some sketches. Bring them to me tomorrow."

"Are there other pieces in the room that I can see, sir? So that I can design a piece that would be fitting?"

"Pull the drawings for the last three pieces we've done for royals. This one is headed to the same place."

"Sir?"

"It seems that Queen Victoria is not pleased with the reflection in the dressing mirror she has."

"Begging your pardon, sir, but I don't believe a new mirror will change the reflection."

Mr. Morris tried to stifle back a smile. He looked up at Thomas.

"That, my friend, is the challenge of the design."

Thomas drew into the night. He was quite familiar with Victorian style, as most of the pieces that William Morris made were of this genre. The lines were more curved, ornate, and many of the pieces looked as if they were French court pieces, although some designers were experimenting with inlays, marbles, and metals. Many prominent London families copied the styles for their own furnishings, while adding other details.

A piece commissioned for the queen, however, or any member of the royal family, had to bear the crown and "HRH" insignia somewhere on the facing wood. Only pieces that were commissioned and then later certified by a commissioner of her court were considered to be authentic Victorian furnishings. Although, generally, all pieces that were being made were referred to as Victorian period pieces.

Thomas had the facing design quite clearly detailed in his mind, but the challenge of providing a "flattering" reflection was creating a challenge for him. After experimenting with various shapes of mirrored glass, he had concluded that an oval shape, with a beveled edge, provided the cleanest lines around the shape of the human body. But a heavy wood frame seemed to accentuate the waist and hips, and this seemed to be contrary to his objective.

So he set about to take an oval-shaped glass and inlay it into another shape frame. A square created too much heaviness in the wood to the corners, but a rectangular shape elongated the mirror and yet left room for the royal insignias in each of the corners. In fact, he could thin the frame down to no more than an inch or so at the two widest points of the oval and, by doing so, draw the attention of the eye either up or down to the darker corners and thus away from the body's midsection. The eyes would be drawn either to the face or the legs, as opposed to the midsection.

At each of the four corners, he placed the queen's insignia, the three-point crown with the letters "HRH" below.

He presented the design to Mr. Morris the next day, drawn from three different perspectives. He described the effect of the shape of the frame and of the glass on the reflection. Mr. Morris nodded silently. The marriage of two shapes effecting the reflection in the mirror was quite interesting to Mr. Morris, and he was eager to see if it were true.

"I'd like to see a model of this, to test your assumptions on the shape and its impact on the reflection. Once you have created a model, we will see if your assumptions prove correct."

Thomas began the work in earnest, using a soft pinewood. He discovered that by altering the weight in the corners, the reflection did indeed change. He also discovered that by elongating the oval, or conversely widening it, the reflection changed dramatically.

He worked diligently for most of the day, taking time in the afternoon to plane a wardrobe he was working on and to turn the legs of a Louis XV chair. At the end of the day, before he put away his tools for the evening, he leaned the mirror upright against the wall and covered it loosely with canvas. He was anxious to begin the work in the morning

As he walked to the shop the next morning, he stopped at every store window to stare at his reflection. The difference in the reflection varied dramatically depending on two factors: the amount of light both in front and behind the reflection and the size of the reflecting glass itself. Too large or too small and the reflection was distorted. Too dark or too light and the reflection was not true to color. Thomas was pondering this as he arrived at the shop and noticed that another apprentice had removed the canvas and was studying the mirror.

"I'd be most appreciative if you didn't disturb that. I've used a very soft pine, and it will dent and crack easily if it is moved around."

"Sorry. I was wanting to get at the planer behind it." Thomas noticed that the spot he had leaned it on was indeed blocking the small planer that was used for turning table legs and other small pieces.

"I didn't notice that I had blocked that. I apologize."

The canvas had already been removed, and as the two men began to lift the mirror, Thomas made an amazing discovery. The filtered light coming in from the windows at the top of the workshop completely changed the light in the reflection in the mirror. Just as he had noticed on his walk to the shop this morning, the amount of light on the mirror changed the complexion and look of what it was reflecting. Thomas's hair, a sandy brown when looking directly at the mirror, turned a softer, lighter shade with the light's reflection above him.

He experimented all day, moving the mirror around the shop, turning it at different angles at different times of day to record the varying colors and images. Could it be possible to create a mirror that could capture all the idiosyncrasies of light and space to create a perfect reflection? If he could, then the reflection could be changed, and most certainly, it could be enhanced.

The theory excited Thomas, and he ran to Mr.

Morris to share his ideas.

"Most unusual, although it makes perfect sense. I suppose I have never thought of the possibilities because the mirrors are always affixed to a wall or a permanent object such as a wardrobe or sideboard. If we could make the mirror free to move, then it could be adjusted to suit the desires of the person reflected in it."

It was at that moment that Thomas knew what he needed to do. He bored a hole at the each side of the mirror at the widest point in the oval, the narrowest part of the frame. He affixed two bolts, one to each side of the frame to create two "pins." To each of these pins he would build a standing base that would allow the mirror to be pivoted back and forth, and enable the amount of light cast on the reflection to be changed to suit the person using the mirror—in effect, to capture the perfect reflection no matter what time of day or where in the room. It would also allow the mirror to be moved around in the room, since the base would be free standing. So depending on the season and the direction of the sun, the mirror could capture more or less light.

He showed the design to Mr. Morris, who was quite pleased.

"I shouldn't think there is really a way to change the reflection the queen casts, but you have certainly created an environment that may allow her to think so."

It was spectacular in all respects. The other craftsmen in Morris's shop all shared in the "genius" of the free-standing mirror that Thomas had created. They stood and marveled at the change in the reflection with just the slightest change to the position in the base. They moved the mirror from one place to another to see what light from different directions did to the image in the mirror. It was, they all agreed, quite an innovative achievement.

The mirror was to be delivered on Tuesday morning. Thomas spent the better part of Monday, reapplying wood oils and polishing the mirror. The glass artisan that had worked with Thomas had also done a masterful job. In keeping with the carvings of the wood along the heavier sides of the frame, the beveled edge of the mirror had been finely etched in the pattern of a vine. The etching was so delicate, it could only be seen at certain angles.

The crown carvings in each of the four corners were perfectly shaped and measured to be exact matches on all four corners. It stood, from base to top almost seven feet tall. Thomas would hold his breath until he knew the response of the queen. Surely she would be pleased. He brought his intended, Margaret, down to the shop on Monday afternoon to see the piece, and she thought it quite something.

"Imagine, a mirror that can make you look better than you actually do!" she exclaimed, when Thomas showed her the various angles and patterns. He thought her reflection to be quite lovely no matter what angle he held the mirror, and he told her so.

"How fortunate that you do not need this to look lovely, my dear."

By midday on Tuesday, Thomas knew something was wrong and began to feel uneasy. Mr. Morris left hours ago and should surely have returned by now. The other artisans tried to assuage his discomfort by telling him that they were sure it was so well received that Mr. Morris was detained in taking commissions for more pieces. Thomas appreciated their efforts to improve his mood, but he was still worried. What if the piece was refused? What if the pivot bolts hadn't held? Without knowing the dynamics of the light in the room, how could he be certain that the mirror would perform as it had in the shop?

As he was fretting over these thoughts, Mr. Morris arrived back at the shop. Thomas could see the canvas covering something in the back of the wagon. His heart sunk. She had not liked it.

Mr. Morris entered the shop and approached Thomas slowly. His face said everything. He looked at Thomas and began.

"Her Majesty the Queen regrets to inform you that while the design of the mirror is particularly stunning and sets a particularly fine reflection, the cherry wood is not to her liking. The mirror is be remade in mahogany."

Thomas did not know what to think. Cherry wood had been requested; they had built it in cherry wood.

But the design had won her over. The floating mirror was a success.

"Thomas," said Mr. Morris, "everything starts with an idea. The idea is sound. The design is good. Her taste in woods notwithstanding, the mirror is an excellent piece. I am proud of this work and you should be as well."

Thomas knew he was right, but he so desperately wanted it to be a success. He thought it might give him the freedom to do some of his own works, to build his own reputation based on his own style. He'd have to be more patient, he thought.

"Mr. Morris? Can I speak with you for a moment, sir?" Thomas had knocked lightly before answering to the booming "come in!"

"Well, sir, I plan to finish up with the mahogany mirror tomorrow. I thought you would like to know so you can check the piece and arrange a time for delivery."

"Yes, and are you pleased with the mirror, Thomas?"

"Yes, sir. Although, between you and me, sir, I prefer the cherry wood myself." He smiled slightly.

"Yes, well, we mustn't get too attached to an idea, now, must we? Good design is the ability to let an idea take shape, change form. This is how design is done." He paused briefly to judge Thomas's reaction to the words. "Well, thank you for letting me know when the mirror will be ready."

"Yes, sir." Thomas continued standing in Mr. Morris's office.

"Was there something else, Thomas?"

"Yes, sir. I have been meaning to ask you about something. What will you be doing with the first mirror, sir? The cherry one?"

"Well, I'll use it as a model, a sample, I suppose. Why?"

"Sir, would you be willing to let me purchase it? I can't afford to pay what the queen would, but I can pay a fair price that would more than cover all the materials, and I figure I've already supplied the labor. It would mean a lot to me, sir. I plan to be married next month, and it would make a fine wedding gift. I'd be willing to sand out the royal crowns if you'd like, sir."

Mr. Morris stood silently.

"Let me think on it, Thomas."

Thomas nodded and left the room.

"Mr. Morris is wanting to see you, Thomas," one of the shop boys yelled across the room.

Thomas ran to the office, three steps at a time. He wasn't getting his hopes up, but he was still hoping that Mr. Morris had considered his offer on the mirror.

"Thomas, come in. I've been thinking about your proposal for the cherry mirror, and I think we can both help each other."

"That's good news, sir. How so?"

"How much do you know about Australia, Thomas?"

"I know they have a lot of kangaroos and British prisoners, sir."

Mr. Morris laughed. Thomas was startled by it.

Although Thomas had always described Mr. Morris as a kind enough man, he couldn't recall ever having heard him laugh.

"Well, they also have a rising population of settlers. Some quite wealthy, from England and other places in Asia and Europe. They have a rising trade with other countries, and I've been thinking it might be a good opportunity to expand William Morris Artisans to a new territory. I'd like you to go and represent us. You'd be working for me, but a certain percentage of proceeds would be yours, and," he added quickly, "the mirror will be yours to keep.

"In addition, as the business grows and you bring on other craftsmen, proceeds from their works would be strictly yours to divide. I would travel over with you, help you get started and settled, and then come back to England after about six months or so."

Mr. Morris watched Thomas's face, hoping to glean some emotion, but Thomas was a hard one to read. Mr. Morris had learned that over the years of watching him. He kept his feelings to himself, and trying to discern what he was thinking was a little like reading tea leaves. Even if you thought you might know which way he was headed, a slight change in direction had a great impact on the outcome.

"You think about it. I'd like to know by the end of the week. I'll have to choose someone else if you decide it's not for you."

Thomas thanked him and told him he'd have to speak with Margaret. It would be hard for her to leave her family here, but he would convince her it was the right thing to do. A chance to run his own shop! To do his own designs! He would never see that here. He headed to the door. When on the other side, he turned and knocked lightly.

"Yes, Thomas, have you left something?"

"No, sir. I've thought about your offer. When do I leave?"

Margaret Brown met Thomas Smyth when she was fifteen years old. Her father, an officer in the Royal Navy, had requested William Morris to craft a dining table for his growing family. Margaret's mother had given birth to six children, and Mr. Brown thought it time to all be seated at the same table.

The table William Morris crafted was simple—an extension type, to expand or contract as necessary. The Browns were not particularly social, but entertained on occasion, and Mrs. Brown wanted to be able to accommodate a party of twelve comfortably. It was crafted of walnut, a deep brown, almost black, and had lighter mahogany inlays, four quarter panels that were prominent when the table was at its natural size.

The table was delivered by Mr. Morris himself and two of his young apprentices. Margaret peered around the corner of the dining room to watch the table being brought into the dining room. But the table was not her primary interest. One of Mr. Morris's apprentices caught her attention from the moment she saw him in the wagon, peeling off the canvas covers.

He was older than she, probably seventeen or eighteen she guessed. He had sandy blond hair and fair skin, and the sleeves on his jacket had been turned back to reveal muscular, lean forearms. But she found herself drawn to his hands. As he carefully lowered the table after carrying it from the wagon, his long fingers wrapped around the edges and he gently lowered it to the floor. His hands were beautiful. The fingers were long and shapely, and she guessed the undersides of his hands were filled with calluses and cuts from the wood shop, even though the backsides were smooth and tan.

Once the table had been lowered to the floor, the boy dropped to his knees and crawled under it, beginning to adjust the small weights underneath to make sure it was properly balanced. He then turned each leg ever so slightly in either direction to assure himself that it was sitting completely flat on the floor. Margaret couldn't imagine the table ever moving, given its size, but she was fascinated by the attention to detail. Mr. Morris had the reputation for treating each piece of furniture as a work of art. Her father had told her that some pieces took up to half a day to settle properly. As she watched the young man in front of her, she secretly hoped this would be the same.

Thomas noticed Margaret as well. Or rather, he noticed her noticing him. From the moment their eyes met when he turned from the back of the wagon, she hadn't taken them off of him. *What was she doing?* he wondered. Surely she has all sorts of little navy sires showing her attention. And he was sure that her parents wouldn't approve of him, a furniture apprentice. He found himself distracted, but he couldn't discern whether he was distracted by her or the thought of her watching his every move. He forced himself to concentrate on the task at hand, although he had to admit, drawing out the time there did have some appeal.

"Margaret, stop standing in the way of things!" her father bellowed. "Can't you see these boys have work to do? They can't get around to all the legs with you standing there blocking the path."

"I'm sorry, Father," she dropped her eyes to the floor, "and also to you, Mr. Morris. I was just interested to know how exactly the piece is leveled without a leveling tool."

"Well, if you're interested and your father doesn't mind you getting down on your knees, I can show you how it is done. We do use a leveling tool when we are through, but a good artisan can feel if the piece is level, usually with his eyes closed."

She glanced at her father, seeking permission and, although she could tell by the look on his face he wasn't pleased with the idea, he nodded slightly.

She dropped to her knees and looked beneath the table. The boy was lying on his back with his eyes staring at the underside of the table, both hands around one leg, twisting it back and forth ever so gently. The muscles of his hands rose and fell each time he changed direction.

"Each leg sits on a pin that extends into the table. There is only one point at which it fits exactly onto the pin and square with the tabletop. By rotating the table leg back and forth gently, the leg will lock into place, guaranteeing a level surface."

"Does it make a sound when it finds its place?" she inquired.

"It doesn't need to. You can feel it in your hands," the boy replied to her before Mr. Morris could finish.

"Miss Brown, this is one of my apprentices, Thomas Smyth. I apologize for his impertinence."

Mr. Morris scowled at Thomas, and Thomas knew he would get a dressing down back at the shop. No one except Mr. Morris was to speak to a customer, least of all his or her beautiful daughter.

"Oh, no need to apologize. It's nice to make your acquaintance, Mr. Smyth." She lowered her eyes as she spoke. She was fearful if Mr. Morris saw their eyes meet, he would become suspicious.

"Mr. Morris, if you could come to the study, we can arrange settlement," Mr. Brown said, as he came in from the drawing room. "The table and chairs are exquisite, and my wife quite agrees. You have done fine work."

Mr. Morris followed him into his study, leaving Thomas and Margaret alone in the dining room. The other boy returned to the wagon and was folding canvasses.

Margaret's heart was beating so fast she was certain Thomas could hear it even from the six-foot distance she was sitting. She wanted to speak to him but was tongue-tied and anxious.

"Can I offer you something to drink?" she stammered.

"No, miss, thank you. I've almost finished here, " he replied, becoming flushed as the words came out of his mouth and he met her gaze. He was almost hoping that one of the pins would break off and he would have to stay longer to repair it, but they had been perfectly turned. He knew that, because he had turned the legs himself.

My, she is lovely, he thought. Her eyes were a beautiful delft blue, almost the color of a hyacinth, and her skin was pale and so translucent, it glowed. He noticed that the light coming in from the windows behind her created a halo around her head and shoulders. He wasn't sure how old she was, although he assumed she was younger than he by a few years.

As Thomas was just setting the last leg, Mr. Morris returned to the room.

"Will you be finishing up here, Thomas?"

"Yes, sir. I'm on the last leg now, sir. Shouldn't be more than a few minutes."

Margaret's heart fell. She knew she would have no occasion to see him again. Furniture was not something her mother and father purchased on a weekly basis.

As her mind raced with thoughts of how she would be able to see him again, Thomas was packing the toolbox. He moved slowly toward the wagon with Mr. Morris and her father.

"Thank you again, Lieutenant Colonel Brown. I hope you and your family enjoy its use and have many happy times around it."

Margaret stood at the door and watched the wagon slowly pull away. She and Thomas's eyes locked until the wagon rounded the corner and he was out of sight.

She thought she might burst into tears when she turned to close the door behind her father, but she regained her composure and followed him back to the dining room.

"A handsome piece, don't you think, Margaret? I am sure that we will enjoy many happy hours around it."

"Yes, Father."

She lowered her eyes as she spoke, and that's when she saw it. Under the table, where he had turned the last leg, a glistening piece of metal caught the light and shone directly in her eye. She didn't move for fear her father might notice it as well. When he finally left the room, she dove to the floor to pick it up. It was a slender piece of metal with a thin wood handle, wider at the bottom and tiny at the top, almost like the point of a needle. She had noticed him using it on the last leg, but she had no idea what it was for.

Well, she thought to herself slyly, *this shall certainly have to be returned to its owner.* She would tell no one for fear of someone else taking it back to Mr. Morris. *No,* she thought, *I will find a way to do it myself.*

Margaret recalled this as clearly as if it had happened yesterday. And now, after three years of courting, having reached her eighteenth birthday, her father had consented to give her hand in marriage. Although the union was not well received at first, her parents had grown to love Thomas and knew that he loved their daughter. His career progressed with Mr. Morris and he had become quite a fine artisan. Many of London's high social circles had heard the name of Thomas Smyth and some had commissioned pieces by him. He had developed a fine eye for design and the quality of his woodworking was truly exceptional. Mr. Morris touted him as his finest apprentice and had shared with Mr. Brown privately that he hoped to make him a partner some day.

"Margaret, it's what I've been hoping for since the first day I walked into Mr. Morris's shop. It's an opportunity I will never have here as long as I'm in his shadow. In Australia, I can run my own shop, build my own book of business. Build a life for us."

"What's wrong with our life here? Why can't you do it here? My family is here, Thomas, my mother, my sisters. What will I do? How will I raise a family without them?"

"We can be a family, Margaret. We can build our own family together. This is important to me, and I want to go. I'll never have the kind of independence I want if I stay here. This opportunity is an incredible gift, and I can't let it go by."

"Well, I want to stay in London," she replied coldly. "I think you should go home now. I need to think about this."

He brushed her cheek gently and turned from the room. He bid a hasty good-bye to her mother, who had been standing in the dining room. He knew, from the look on her face, she had heard every word. Margaret's mother had always liked him, but he feared this would change all that.

"Mr. Morris has asked him to start a shop in Australia. He wants to leave right after we are married." She didn't face her mother but, instead, continued staring out the window even though he was long out of view.

"That's preposterous. Does he have any idea what he is asking of you? Taking you from your home, your family?"

"Mother, when you married father, he had already received his commission in the Royal Navy. You knew you wouldn't stay in one place for the rest of your life."

"That was different. I knew I'd never leave England."

"Yes, but he's left you countless times since you have been married, on one duty or another. He left the day after John was born and didn't come back for two years. I'm not sure I see a difference."

"The difference was that we had a home here. He might have been on the open seas without us, but he always came home to this house."

"Mother, what kind of a home was it without him in it?"

Her mother sighed and walked to the window. They did not look at one another, but both stared out onto the gray street below.

"Do you love him, Margaret? Can you be without him?"

She closed her eyes and pressed her cheek and hand to the cold window. "I cannot breathe without him mother."

"Then you've already made your choice." She rested her hand gently on Margaret's shoulder and continued looking straight ahead. "And you have chosen him."

She walked slowly to the shop. The package was heavy, and she was thankful that the meat markets were not too far from Mr. Morris's shop. Margaret had seen the advertisement in the paper and thought it might be a good way to tell him what she had decided. She knew he would go, with her or without her. Truth be told, the more she thought about it, the more the idea grew on her. The bone-chilling January cold in London was making her weary. It had been sixty-four days without a ray of sunshine, and it was depressing her. The idea of warm, sunny temperatures and beaches you could actually stand on without being blown to bits was appealing.

She knocked lightly.

"Mr. Morris," she said, "may I speak with Thomas for a moment?"

Mr. Morris looked at the package she was carrying.

"Last supper?" he said, and smiled at her gently. He was anxious for Thomas to leave for Australia, but he was uncertain as to whether or not she would be accompanying him. Thomas told him that she was not eager to go, but he was hopeful he could convince her. Either way, he said, he would go. With her or without her.

"Not my intention," she said in a startled tone, "but that will depend on whether or not he likes the food, I suspect."

Mr. Morris laughed out loud. He liked Margaret, always had. He had known her since she was a young girl, when he had done his first piece for Colonel Brown.

"He's in the kiln room, drying. Watch the bottom of your skirt, miss. Wouldn't want it to catch a spark."

"Thank you."

She made her way through the shop, averting the eyes of most of the other apprentices. It wasn't often a woman came through here. Since Thomas had been asked by Mr. Morris to take on the new venture in Australia, she sensed some tension. When she reached the kiln room, she could see Thomas through the seam of the door, running his hands along a piece of wood. His eyes were closed and his hands were doing all the work. When he came to a rough spot, he would chalk it, and then continue on. When he had finished the length of the board, he would apply more heat to the chalked spots, one at a time.

"I've brought you lunch. Something you haven't tried before but I thought you might find interesting," she said coming through the doorway.

"That was thoughtful of you," Thomas said, surprised. "Guess I'm not in too much trouble, then?"

"I wouldn't be so quick to draw that conclusion. Maybe you should decide on that after you've eaten." She wanted to be stern, but it was impossible. He looked at her, and she smiled. "Open it."

Thomas unwrapped the string and opened the butcher paper to see what looked like a raw piece of meat. Although it had the texture of beef, it was an odd color, something between brown and gray, almost the color of gravy.

"I think you might have forgotten to cook it."

"Oh, no, it's been cooked. At least that's what they told me it would look like cooked."

He took a small bite to test the flavor. He nodded slightly and gave a look to her that indicated that at least it was edible.

"I hope you like it, Thomas, because we're going to be eating a lot of it, I'm afraid." She continued watching his face and, after a moment, burst out laughing. "It's kangaroo meat, Thomas. It arrived off the S.S. *Great*

Britain this morning, refrigerated the whole way from Sydney."

He dropped the package to the ground and embraced her.

"I will make you so happy, I promise you," he said.

I do not understand her yet. She is a bit of a mystery to me. Her image seems so vacant, but surely there is something there. Has she always been this guarded, or did she become this way over time? When she stares blankly in this direction, she is always more interested in the reflection of something else. I think she is afraid of what she will see if she really looks. She has been so careful to create the image that the outside sees.

What lies beneath?

Beth—2002

"Jeff Hancock is holding for you," Kim said with a tone of exasperation. She knew that he and Beth had exchanged at least four phone calls, and Kim was running out of pleasantries.

"And he would be . . . ?" Beth was clearly distracted.

"Your mirror man."

"Oh, right. God, I am totally losing it." She ran back to her office and picked up.

"Hi, Mr. Hancock. Thanks so much for returning my phone calls. I apologize. I've been hard to get a hold of.

"It's Jeff, please. No problem. I usually expect at least three meaningful conversations with a person's voice mail before I actually speak with them."

She smiled to herself. *A sense of humor*, she thought. *That's good.*

"How can I help you?"

"My husband and I just bought a house out at Stinson Beach."

"Lucky you. Congratulations. A weekend place then?"

"Well, I'm actually going to try and telecommute, if I can get Pacific Bell to put a DSL line out there."

"Well, that sounds highly civilized."

"We'll see if I can make it work. Always sounds good in theory. Listen, the reason for my call is that I need to have someone take a look at an old mirror. It's in the house and can't be moved."

"Uh-huh."

"It was part of the deal with the house. The previous owner wants it in that location, ad infinitum."

"Okay, my curiosity is piqued. Is there something unusual about it?"

"That's what I'm hoping you can tell me. It's a decorating nightmare, but the thing is, it's kind of growing on me. I'm hoping it can be cleaned up a bit, refinished maybe. Maybe stripped down to the original wood, something like that. So I was hoping you might be able to take a look."

"Well, I don't actually do any restoration. I can tell you about it, how old it is, if it's worth anything, but I'd have to refer you to someone for restoration."

"That's fine. I'm just looking for somewhere to start."

"Okay. When's a good time for me to come take a look? Since it can't be moved, I'll be driving out to see it?"

"Right. It's best if you see it in daylight. How about Thursday morning, about nine-thirty?"

She could hear him typing on a keyboard in the background. How busy could a furniture appraiser be?

"Thursday morning is good. Directions?"

"Take One to Old Coast Road and make a left, then right onto Dune. We're at 16 Dune Lane. Ugly green color. Take the driveway all the way down to the porch."

"Okay. See you Thursday at nine-thirty."

He pulled up in a Jeep Cherokee, so Beth was expecting an outdoorsy sort. When a slight man, decidedly the nonoutdoorsy type, got out of the car, she was surprised. *Hmmm,* she thought, *definitely not what I expected from the phone.*

But the voice matched, the minute he said hello, and she recognized the same hint of sarcasm.

"Gee, I'd love to put your DSL line in lady, but you'll need a phone first."

Beth laughed out loud.

"Yes, this end of the road is a little rustic," she said.

"That's probably why you like it." He smiled as he climbed the steps to the door.

He walked through the house slowly. The back entry was so awkward, Beth thought. If and when they remodeled this place, she thought, that was the first thing to be changed. They lived to the front of the house, and yet, the "front" entry on the driveway was narrow, dark, and nothing more than a hallway to get you into the rest of the house. Maybe they could move the entry to the side?

"Well, there it is. Charming, huh?" She pointed to the mirror with an outstretched hand. The place was still empty, and Beth thought it looked even more unsightly than when they had looked at the house.

"Oh, I don't know. It's a little sixties decoupage-looking, but I can tell already, it has good bones. May I?" he asked as he pulled it down from the wall.

"Be my guest." Beth was taking in what the wall looked like without it. Blank.

He removed a small penknife from his bag and turned the mirror over.

"I'll try to see what I can from the back, that way you won't have any facing marks. But I may have to leave a few scratches in the front if I can't get what I need from back here. Okay?"

"Don't worry about it. As I said, I'm going to refinish it if the wood is any good. If not, I'll paint it for sure. That green is bad."

"Must have liked green. It's the same color as the house." Beth hadn't realized it until he said it. But then she thought, and the tile in the big bathroom and all of the appliances, outside furniture, everything. Monochromatic green.

He ran his hands over the front and sides, stopping for a moment at the widest point. He scraped a little of the paint off with a fingernail.

"The wood underneath is cherry. Looks a little bruised in some spots, but cherry is a good hard wood, and stuff that was made out of it was built to last. Toned up, it's really quite rich looking."

He peeled a little more paint, at the narrowest part of the frame, the widest point of the oval. He seemed very interested in this area. He ran his hands back and forth, closed his eyes for a moment. Then he turned the mirror on its side. Or so she thought.

"This mirror was actually meant to hang vertically. It was made as a dressing mirror probably. There are wood pinholes in the sides, but the wood pins have been sheared off and sanded down. It probably was pivoted to some sort of base at one point in its lifetime, but it's been removed."

Beth got closer and ran her hands over the frame. In this position, she could see the carvings in the corners more clearly. The detail, although badly covered by the paint was coming through as he scraped.

"Well, I'll be damned," he said.

He used his penknife to gently scrape off one entire corner, and then looked at Beth with a sort of guilty expression. He'd gotten a little carried away and all of the paint was entirely gone on the one corner.

"You said you wanted to refinish it, right?" he said sheepishly.

"I'll be damned, what?" Beth was wondering what was so interesting to him. "Have I got a priceless antique?" Beth asked, her voice dripping with sarcasm.

"Priceless, no. Expensive, yes. Do you see these carvings in the four corners?" Beth looked carefully. She had noticed the carvings in the corners were the same pattern, symmetrical. But with the mirror now standing on end, she noticed that in all four corners of the mirror was a small crown, crosshatched where the points of the crown reached up, and underneath, in script, the letters "HRH."

"This was crafted for a royal. Probably Victoria. She had a big ego. In the late nineteenth century, any furnishing, carpeting, drapery—anything—had to bear the royal insignia—queen's orders."

"So this thing is one hundred and fifty years old?"

"Somewhere between one hundred and two hundred. She was the longest reigning royal. Ruled for almost the entire nineteenth century." He paused and intently studied the crown patterns. "But what's really interesting is the crosshatch in the crown points."

"Why so?" Beth asked.

"I have read that occasionally a piece got made for the Queen and when it was done, she decided she didn't care for it. Couldn't sell it with the crowns in it, so the artisan would crosshatch either the crown or the HRH."

"Would they try to resell them?"

"Not likely. Usually the artisan paid for the materials and kept them, either for display or in their own homes."

"Kind of like a second?"

"Something like that. Although anyone who would have seen this would have known that's what it was," he paused for a moment and then added, "The mirror has been replaced. This isn't the original glass."

"How can you tell?"

"Mirrored glass back then had a bevel, to hold it into the frame. Do you see the lip around the edge of this wood? The bevel was fitted into that lip so the mirror wouldn't fall out. This glass doesn't have the bevel. It's been cut to fit the hole, but probably glued on so it doesn't fall out. That makes the mirror less valuable, but the original glass was probably so bad, you couldn't see anything in it."

"So it could be stripped back to the cherry? Could the carvings be brought out?"

"It could definitely be returned to its original wood tone, but I wouldn't alter the carvings. I think a good restorer could clean them up, make them pop out a bit more, but I'd be cautious about deepening them. More likely for someone to think it's a fake."

"How do you know it isn't?" she said quizzically.

He turned the mirror on its side again and motioned for her to get closer.

At the side of the frame, about where the wood pins were for what had once been a stand was the inscription "William Morris, 1881" and below that were even smaller initials, "TES."

"William Morris was quite a furniture artisan in London in the mid-eighteen hundreds. Did pieces for the royal family, high society types mostly. TES is probably an apprentice who did this one."

"So, it's worth restoring then?"

"If I had to look at it as much as you do, I'm not sure I'd worry about the money. I'd be more concerned with restoring it and enjoying it. I'd be intrigued to know where it's been, how it got here." He paused and sighed gently. "But that's just me. Part of what I like about what I do is that I find myself inside a story. Every piece of furniture is part of a family, part of a history. That mirror has a story to tell, and if I owned it, I'd try to find out what it is. Victorian England is a long way from twenty-first-century America."

"Robert Allen is calling for you," whispered Kim. "I think he wants the house back. Says he heard you defaced the mirror and he's suing."

"Very funny. Don't you have work to do?" She picked up the phone as Kim was still giggling.

"Mr. Allen, thanks so much for returning my call."

"My pleasure, Beth. I hope there isn't a problem of some sort. Your message sounded rather urgent."

"No, no. Nothing with the house. It's great. We're trying to settle in, you know." She paused, wondering whether or not she should even be bringing this up. She took a deep breath. "I know I asked you this before, but I was wondering if there is anything else about that mirror you can remember. I had an appraiser come out and look at it. Did you know it was made for a royal—in 1881?"

"Really? Wonder how it ended up in Thea's house. She's not a royal descendant as far as I know." He laughed slightly.

"You mentioned that your mother might remember something."

"I think I also mentioned she has Alzheimer's disease. I'm not sure she'd be of much help."

"Just the same, I'd like to try. If you don't mind."

"She lives at the Kent Woodlands Home. She is always interested in a visitor. But don't get your hopes up," he quickly added. "Is investigating a hobby?"

"No. Actually, I do plenty of investigating during the week. Let's just say I'm naturally intellectually curious."

"Good luck with your hunt."

"Thank you. I'll be in touch."

It is unhappiness. Unhappiness brought about by loneliness. I am glad to have no use for emotion, I merely observe. What causes emotion to have such power, such control? I wonder. It appears that they are powerless to change them, these feelings. I see the peaks and valleys and wonder, how can it be that the variability does not break them? That the highs and lows do not suck them under, like a powerful wave? Still, they rise against all odds and face yet more. I think there must be nothing more powerful than the human spirit.

With all its frailties, still it rises.

Margaret—1881–1884

The S.S. *Great Britain* was the largest ship in the world when it was launched in 1852 for its maiden voyage to Sydney. It was the first ship to be driven by a propeller and the first to have an iron hull. At capacity, it held slightly over 600 passengers in three classes. Mr. Morris had arranged for Thomas and Margaret to be accommodated in first class, a luxury that Thomas could not have afforded on his own. But Mr. Morris, having created quite a fine reputation and a fine income for himself, wanted Thomas and his new bride to be comfortable for the crossing. It would be a journey of almost five weeks, longer if they were held at Quarantine Station.

    They embarked on February 12, 1881, one of the S.S. *Great Britain*'s last few voyages. The ship was retired later that year, after more than twenty-five trips between Sydney, Melbourne, and London. Mr. Morris accompanied them, given Thomas knew little of actually setting up a shop, or a household for that matter, and Mr. Morris wanted desperately to see Australia. He planned on staying several months to get things established and then depart in the fall. Thomas sensed that Mr. Morris was aching for this trip, yearning for something new.

    They enjoyed the journey immensely. None of them complained of seasickness, and the opulence afforded them in first class was spectacular. Livestock was actually penned below so that first-class passengers could have fresh meat and dairy for their journey. A feature that astounded Thomas. He concluded that he was living better these five weeks than his previous twenty-two years.

The trip took a little less than five weeks, and on the morning of March nineteenth when they awoke they could see the North and South Heads of Sydney's Harbor rising to greet them. Just beyond the North Head, they could see the outline of Quarantine Station. After four and a half weeks, Margaret was bursting with excitement to have actually arrived. She would be bitterly disappointed if they were detained at Quarantine Station for any longer than absolutely necessary. She had heard stories of ships berthed for days when influenza was discovered.

Most of the passengers had made their way to a deck or window, peering at the landscape. *Were they looking for similarities to or differences from the home they had left behind,* Thomas wondered. Mr. Morris, Thomas, and Margaret stood on the starboard side and watched Australia rise up before them. The entrance to the harbor was an awesome sight. The three of them stood in complete silence as the thundering heads loomed larger and larger. The ship let out a shrill whistle, indicating it would be anchoring soon, just short of the harbor entrance at Quarantine Station. They knew they had time to gather belongings and prepare for disembarking, but Margaret was growing anxious and returned to their room.

Most of their personal belongings were still in their room, while their furnishings and larger items were held in berths below. But Margaret had insisted on the mirror staying in the room with them. She feared it might be damaged and she couldn't bear the thought. Her wedding gift from Thomas had become her most prized possession. She had seen a free-standing mirror once before, but it was small and intended for being situated on a tabletop. When Thomas recounted the story to her about its making, she felt a chill go up her spine. His description of the design and the pattern had left her feeling as though he really was the most creative and passionate of people. To most people, it was a piece of furniture. To Thomas, it was something created to reflect the soul.

She knew the mirror had been commissioned for the queen, and she was surprised that Mr. Morris had not asked for the crowns to be sanded out of the four corners. He said that since he knew it would not be resold, Thomas needed only to crosshatch the crowns. Most people would think it was part of the design. That way, he felt it would be a nice display piece for their new shop in Australia.

Margaret hoped that would not mean it would leave her home. She had already spoken to Thomas about using their home for display, as Thomas had crafted some beautiful pieces, including a wardrobe and an exact copy of the dining table and chairs in her parents' house—the table that had brought them together. Thomas had gotten Mr. Morris's permission to stay in the shop late at night, to purchase his own materials, and to craft several pieces for their new home. The condition from Mr. Morris was that the pieces be freely available for potential customers to examine.

But the mirror was not wrapped in canvas below. The mirror had watched their journey and would continue to watch their new life as it unfolded.

They passed through Quarantine Station without delay and slowly made their way up the entrance to Sydney Harbor. Although Sydney was clearly visible, Margaret was enthralled with the communities that had been built up along the head areas all the way in to Circular Quay. She would later learn that these were some of the most exclusive areas of Sydney, where many of Thomas's customers would live. There had been fortunes made here in the last two decades from wool and gold.

The great rising dome of the Garden Palace, where Sydney had held its First International Exposition the year before, majestically overlooked the city. It was an awesome structure, made entirely of wood and glass, and Thomas and Mr. Morris were fascinated by it. As they made their way to the hotel down McQuarie Street, Thomas asked the driver to stop so that he could get a closer look. The delay was torturous for Margaret, although she knew that Thomas's creative senses were stirring. He was absorbing the architecture of the building, storing it somewhere in the recesses of his mind. She knew some part of it would reappear in a design later—she could tell by the look on his face. As she stared at him, he signaled the driver to move on, but clearly, he had taken away an idea, a pattern, a shadow, something that stuck with him.

The Royal Australian Hotel was an imposing edifice on McQuarie Street. Built in the 1860s at the height of the gold rush fever in Australia, it was finely detailed and impressively ornate. The metal structure on the exterior actually folded into the interior of the building to form a grand foyer and lobby area, where Margaret found herself standing by all of their belongings loaded onto gleaming brass carts. The mirror was not among them. She panicked momentarily before catching a glimpse of the canvas-wrapped piece, looking vaguely like the outline of a human body. "What must they think we are traveling with?" she muttered to herself, as she watched it ascend into the elevator.

Their room was lovely, overlooking Hyde Park, with a view of St. James Cathedral in the foreground. Although she knew she would be comfortable here, she hoped their stay would be brief. She so wanted to be in a permanent home as soon as possible. She peered across at the park, in full flower of summer, and decided she shouldn't attach herself to the view. Upon opening the window, the fragrance of roses, freshly cut grass, and frangipani blossoms filled the room. She closed her eyes and inhaled deeply and knew this place would be nothing like the London she left behind.

Mr. Morris had already acquired shop space on Oxford Street and was certain that suitable living accommodations could be found for them in one of the nearby communities of Darlinghurst or Woolloomooloo. The shop on Oxford Street was quite to Mr. Morris's liking. There was a large area in the front that could display the works, and the shop area in the back could accommodate at least a half-dozen apprentices. It had two small offices to the rear, one for his use while he was there, later to be used by Thomas, and one for a soon-to-be-hired bookkeeper and purchasing agent.

Mr. Morris knew he would have to hire someone with knowledge of the woodcutters, someone from another furniture maker in Sydney who might want to join a reputable English artisan. He had obtained a list of other furniture craftsmen in Sydney as well as a list of potential clients. His clients in England had provided him introductions to some of the finest families in Sydney. The prime minister, his cabinet, several wealthy sheep station owners, traders, bankers, and the like. He was confident he could begin building a book of business quickly.

While Thomas thought the shop probably appropriate for running a business, the work area did not inspire him. It was dark and largely square—a completely ordinary room, for lack of a better description. But the ceilings were high, and Thomas pondered the potential of replacing some of the wall space toward the roofline with glass panes, to let in natural light and open the area up a bit. He would mention it to Mr. Morris when he found the right time. At the moment, Mr. Morris was already starting lists of tasks. He asked Thomas to begin the list of equipment and then gave him the addresses of several toolmakers in the vicinity.

"You'll want to meet these people yourself, forge relationships with them. Better for you to take that on than I, as I will not be here to continue them. If the business grows, you will be trading with them frequently. They might also be aware of some woodcraftsmen that might be interested in joining us."

Thomas was an artisan at heart, not a businessman, so the process of initiating business with the tool cutters and die makers was unnatural to him. For the first time since he began working with Mr. Morris, he felt completely out of his element. But he found that once he began to show them the portfolio of designs and to describe what he needed by sharing the drawings and the measurements, he was back at his craft. He secured much of the equipment he needed and was given advice on how and where to get the rest of the tools that he could not find. One toolmaker was particularly helpful in telling him that one of Sydney's design houses just lost their artisan to influenza and the three apprentices might be looking for a new shop.

Mr. Morris and Thomas carried out their duties for the first several weeks, securing all that they needed to be in a position to start looking for customers.

"Thomas, put on your best suit, and bring the book. It is time to find some buyers."

The process of building a book of business was not as difficult as Thomas had thought, although Mr. Morris was doing most of the selling. The previous two decades in Sydney and, for that matter, in all of Australia brought about an explosion of wealth. The railway system opened up Queensland and Western Australia as well as Victoria. Although there was plenty of business to be had in Sydney, Mr. Morris's introductions extended into several of the other colonies as well.

Having been provided introductions by some very prominent British families and loyal customers, no one refused to meet with Mr. Morris, and by the end of the first set of visits, Thomas had secured orders for dining tables, chairs, wardrobes, and two dressing mirrors, like the one he had given to Margaret as her wedding gift. Many of the pieces that had been commissioned for the queen or members of Parliament were requested without hesitation. Mr. Morris's reputation preceded him, and when it was known that many of the designs were in fact Thomas's, the clients were anxious to have Thomas design pieces especially for them.

It was becoming obvious to Mr. Morris and Thomas that they would need to secure at least one other apprentice to assist Thomas, possibly two. The idea that

Thomas was proposing to Mr. Morris was that he would be principally involved in the design of the work and the handling of the clients, and the apprentices would carry out the work. As the apprentices improved, they would take on more of the design work, while Thomas would continue to concentrate on growing the clients. Because of his arrangement with Mr. Morris, all new client work, meaning clients that came without the benefit of Mr. Morris's introduction, would be solely Thomas's income. Clients that Mr. Morris secured during his six-month stay to get the business going would earn Thomas only half. With this arrangement, Thomas was more than eager to build a profitable enterprise, and Mr. Morris knew it.

While the business was getting off to a fine start, Thomas and Margaret's marriage was beginning to show signs of neglect. Thomas seemed singularly focused on getting the business up and running and was eager to be independent of Mr. Morris as soon as possible. Thomas assumed that Margaret was happy here and didn't notice that Margaret was becoming withdrawn and sullen. He noticed she had become quieter but attributed it to her being tired or frustrated over the search for a home. He didn't know that she was, in fact, spending hours in front of her mirror, sobbing until her eyes were swollen shut. And if he knew how bitterly unhappy she was and terribly lonely, he would have convinced himself that once the business was on its own feet, he would give more attention to Margaret and she would be her old self again.

Margaret had never felt so alone in her life. She went from her parents' home, which was always filled with voices and activities from siblings, friends, and neighbors, to a husband she was still getting to know, in a country where she knew no one. There were also very few women in Sydney as compared to the population of men, so making acquaintance with other young women was difficult. In London, her mother had belonged to several ladies social clubs, but when Margaret had inquired about such things here, she was told that nothing like that existed.

Her days seemed excruciatingly long, with Thomas leaving early in the morning and not returning home until late in the evening. Her days were long and dull, the monotony broken only by her excitement at mail delivery time. On the occasion when she received mail from home, she sat all afternoon in the chair in front of the mirror, reading and rereading whatever news she was getting. She sobbed at the thought of her mother so far away. She wrote to her mother and father twice a week. On those days, her writing kept her busy, as she struggled to tell of her excitement over her new life.

But as her letters went on, anyone reading them was certain to know how lonely she had become. She wondered if her mother could tell that her stories were only fabrications of the life she wanted, rather than the one she had. Each letter from her mother asked her to come back home; each letter from Margaret begged her mother to come to Australia.

Finding a suitable place to live was proving to be challenging, and in Margaret's condition of depression, nothing seemed right. Mr. Morris had agreed to help secure their housing with a loan, to be repaid out of Thomas's proceeds, and had also hired a local solicitor to help locate a home. Margaret's tastes were simple, but the solicitor insisted on finding them something grander.

"If your husband is to be a purveyor of fine home furnishings, then you should have a fine home!" he would bellow after Margaret turned down the few homes she was shown.

Finally, after nearly two months of searching, a lovely Victorian brownstone off William Street in Woolloomooloo became home. She had so hoped to find a place with a view of the water and the harbor, but this had a lovely view of Hyde Park from the third floor and would do nicely. She knew just the spot for the mirror.

And for several months, her spirits seemed to improve. She began to settle into their home. She met a few women neighbors, and Thomas thought her mood to be much brighter. Nevertheless, when she asked a third time to take a trip back to London for several months to visit her family, Thomas agreed it might be good for her. Sydney would start getting colder soon, as winter approached, and Thomas thought the change of scenery might renew her enthusiasm once she returned. She would sail in late June, along with Mr. Morris who was planning his return to London.

William Morris & Thomas Smyth, Purveyors of Fine Furnishings was doing exceedingly well with four apprentices and nine under-apprentices. After several months of searching in Sydney to no avail, Mr. Morris sent for his bookkeeper and procurement agent in London to come help Thomas to run the shop. "There is no one I trust more," had said Mr. Morris. "And it will be easier for me to replace him there than to find someone here." He had arrived three weeks earlier and was settled in quite nicely, finding the finest woods and importing when need be. Because of their nearness to the islands of southeast Asia, many tropical woods were available at good prices, and Thomas began to use them extensively. With more help, Thomas was free to focus on the designs and the selling efforts.

Although he had made his own commitment to focus more attention on Margaret, her depression drove him deeper into his work. He hated to admit it, but he knew he was using his work as an excuse to spend as little time with her as possible. She had become so withdrawn, he concluded that she was in a place that he couldn't reach her. He knew he was failing her, but he didn't know what to do for her. The business prospered, and they had more business than they could keep up with as word of mouth continued to bring them new work. And, of course, as the business prospered, Thomas spent less and less time at home. He knew he was a coward for feeling this way, but he was looking forward to her departure for London. If she weren't here with him, he wouldn't have to face the guilt from knowing he had helped to create her misery.

So as Thomas stood at the dock to see them both off, he was a mix of emotions. Dear friend, as well as beloved spouse, both leaving him behind. And although he tried to force the thoughts from his mind, he couldn't help but wonder if he would see either of them again. He wanted Margaret back desperately, but only if she was the woman he married, not this shell he was watching walk away.

Before boarding, Mr. Morris turned to Thomas and shook his hand.

"Thomas, you don't know it yet, but you are going to be more successful than you have ever imagined. You possess a soul that can see possibility. You have a spirit for creating things that can coexist with the human form, and that is something that few men possess. I am proud to call you my partner."

"I will never be able to thank you for all that you have given me, all that you have taught me," Thomas replied.

"You already had it all inside of you, Thomas. I just helped you let it go."

Thomas missed Margaret terribly, more so than he thought he would when she boarded the ship. He would arrive home at night to a still, cold, dark home. He had been distressed that Margaret had become so withdrawn from him, but with her gone he began to realize that he had driven her away. He realized that he didn't really know how to be a good husband to her. He would sit in their bedroom late at night and stare at the dressing mirror he had given her, closing his eyes to imagine her reflection in it. She, too, loved to experiment with the light and darkness of the reflection. She had put the mirror near the window for a time because she thought the light streaming from the windows gave a certain glow to her face that seemed to improve her mood. But as the light began to change in the fall, she decided she looked pale and drawn, and so the mirror had been moved to the other side of the room, nearer to the door. It seemed that if she looked beyond it, she could escape her misery.

How many tears from my lovely bride, Thomas thought now as he stared at it, *has this mirror watched?* He sat on the bed, staring blankly, silent tears rolling down his face. He touched her pillow, brought it to his face, and inhaled deeply, closing his eyes and taking in her scent. He had no idea what he would do if she didn't return.

He tried to bury himself in his work, which wasn't hard. Morris-Smyth was continuing to thrive, and almost all the clients now were of his own cultivation. Without noticing it, Thomas had become quite prosperous.

And the time away from each other seemed to be improving both of their moods. Thomas was recommitted to making Margaret's life the one she said she wanted, and he told her so in his letters. He was a different man in his letters. He was passionate and emotional, and Margaret began to remember why she had fallen in love with him. Likewise, her letters to him seemed to indicate an improving emotional state and a better outlook on life in general, as one passage showed in a letter that arrived in late August:

> "How lovely London is in these waning days of summer. I had forgotten. You know that old expression? The one about London having four seasons? There is winter and there is July, August and September. The gardens at Kensington are brilliant. The fragrance of all the flowers stays with you for hours after you have left and swirls around in the air with every breath. The fading away of the day at sunset lingers for such a long time as the pale blue of the horizon turns deeper and deeper until it is finally black and the stars appear. I know it is fleeting, as there are already signs of the onset of fall. The mornings are becoming a little more crisp, like the first bite of an apple, and just today, I noticed the very tips of the high leaves on mother's maples are singed with red. I will watch them every day to see the color move down the tree, like blood draining from a face.
>
> I have enjoyed spending time with mother and the brothers, but I am aching with loneliness for you, and I am missing my home. I think this is the first time I have

ever really thought of it as my home. Isn't it strange, to call Australia home now, after really so brief a time, but I shall. As I knew the moment that I agreed to go with you, I am even more firmly convinced that my home is wherever you are. I have made arrangement for passage and will leave at the end of September. I am longing to see you again.

Yours,
M

She arrived back in Sydney toward the end of October, bringing with her the first real warm wave of the Australian spring. "Ah" she said as the ship rounded the heads and into the harbor, "the warmth of day that a Londoner will never know, even at the peak of summer." She was so anxious with anticipation, she felt a bit flushed and rushed back to her room to make sure all of her belongings were packed and ready to be unloaded. She was glad to have taken the trip to London, for this rush of exhilaration to be returning was worth the journey alone.

New Year's Day brought an absolutely stifling heat to Sydney. Not a breath of wind, even from the sea, could cool the temperature. The breeze coming off the water wasn't cooling in the least, and Margaret complained of being dizzy and lightheaded for several days, even after it finally broke. When she was still nauseous and tired after a week, she called the doctor.

"Well, my dear, nothing serious. Nothing that a few more months of rest won't take care of," he said, beaming a broad smile.

Margaret burst into tears. A baby.

"Oh, it's nothing to cry about."

"Oh, yes, it is. I've never been happier in my life," she said dabbing her eyes with his handkerchief.

"You'll need a fair bit of extra rest. Given your frail nature, I'm going to prescribe bed rest for you. Probably best to take precautions. And if you feel depressed or overly anxious, you need to call me immediately." Margaret's doctor knew something of her previous depression, having seen her several times in the last year.

Margaret left the office a little stunned and slightly euphoric. She decided she would say nothing to Thomas, just in case.

She felt terrible night and day. The doctor assured her it was a good sign and that it meant that her hormones were functioning properly. And as each day passed, Margaret felt more at ease. She also found that as she felt less anxious, she felt less nauseous. More than any other time in her life, she was aware of how connected are the body and the mind. She stared at herself in the mirror every day, looking at her face, her breasts, and her growing belly. She decided she would need to tell Thomas soon, as she wouldn't be able to conceal it for much longer.

Her pregnancy progressed without incident, and Thomas had never been happier. The Margaret he married had returned on that boat, and the impending arrival of the baby seemed to fill Margaret with joy. It was as if he was watching a boat in the harbor, its sails suddenly filled with air. And Margaret felt she suddenly had a life filled with purpose. Thomas loved to stand with her in front of the mirror and put his arms around her mid-section, each day measuring how much tighter the distance was to wrap. Everything about her glowed, and now that she wasn't as tired or as nauseous, for the first time in his married life he couldn't wait to see her at home in the evening.

He was working on a cradle for the baby, to make the days move faster and keep him occupied. It wouldn't be much longer before the cradle would be needed, and he wanted it to be unique. It was a cradle for the baby, but it was also a welcome-back gift for Margaret. He realized in the time that she had been pregnant how close he had come to losing her, and it shook him to the core. The cradle had to be a symbol, not only to celebrate the birth of the baby, but also to remind him of how precious life was.

All of the traditional designs seemed so traditional. He wanted something unique, something lasting. Suddenly, as he sat staring at Margaret and down at the blank piece of paper, he remembered Exposition Hall, the building they had seen the first day they arrived. It had since burned down in a fire, but the lines of the dome and the shape of the curves got him thinking. He tinkered into the early hours of the morning, and when he arrived at the shop the next day, he began the model in earnest. He knew this was it. The headboard and the footboard were to be curved and open, creating a half dome above the baby's head.

As he was beginning to measure the crosspieces and to think about an accompanying piece, a rocker, when one of his young apprentices burst into the office.

"Mr. Smyth, sir, your house girl's out front. Says Miss Margaret is having the baby, sir."

He jumped up and ran to the buggy. Setting the horses on a run, he set out for home. But as he was racing through the streets, he thought, *Too early*. His heart was pumping as he raced up the steps and into the house.

The doctor was in the hallway, his hands wrapped in towels, as their house girl was bringing him a basin of water. The house was eerily quiet, and Thomas noticed the towels were soaked in blood.

The doctor's voice was light.

"Congratulations, Mr. Smyth, you have a little girl," but as he said it, his eyes never met Thomas's gaze.

Thomas was overcome with emotion and fell to his knees in the hallway.

"Can I see her? Can I see Margaret?" He began to take the stairs two at a time, breaking into a run as he reached the landing. When he reached the landing, he turned around and noticed that the water basin the doctor was holding was completely filled with blood.

The doctor turned slowly toward him.

"The baby is fine, Mr. Smyth, but Margaret had a tough time of it, I'm afraid."

Thomas already knew what the doctor was going to tell him. He slumped to the floor and wept.

Why is the letting go so difficult? What pain must there be in setting something free? I have witnessed creation and death in these reflections, and still it is this land between birth and death that creates the most extraordinary tests. While one is filled with excitement and anxiety over what is new, the other is filled with dread. While one looks forward to a new life, the other struggles to look back. It would seem to me that adventures await them both. But while one embraces that idea, the other recoils.

Does he not know that letting go enables both of them to be free?

Anne-Margaret—1902–1906

"I'm telling you, she's too old to be chasing after you at the shop. She needs to experience her own life."

"She does experience her own life," Thomas said in exasperation. This was not the first time he and Mary had had this conversation.

Mary Prescott Tilden was one of Sydney's most prominent rich widows. Thomas Smyth had the good fortune to call her one of his best clients and a dear friend. Over the years, he had completely furnished two of her homes with Thomas Smyth designs and made Thomas Smyth quite wealthy in the process. Mary had also taken on the task of acting as surrogate mother to Thomas's daughter, Anne-Margaret.

"She's nineteen years old, Thomas. You have a grown woman in your house whom you are still treating like one of your shop boys."

"I like having her with me at the shop. Is that so terrible?"

"It's terrible if you are doing it for yourself."

"What does that mean?"

"It means that you can't keep her under your foot forever just so you have company. You have used Anne-Margaret as a replacement for Margaret since the day she was born. It's kept you from loneliness, but it has kept Anne-Margaret from living. You need to let her go, let her explore the world, maybe attend a university somewhere."

"The universities here are not good environments for young women. Too many men."

"I wasn't talking about her going to university here."

"Leave Australia? That's not what she wants."

"I don't think you know what she wants. Have you ever asked her? I think you just assume that she wants what you want for her. She has her mother's strength of character and your desire to succeed. She's not the kind of young woman who's looking to be married off to some Sydney heir-apparent. She needs to find her own way, to live her own life. And so do you."

Thomas stared blankly out the window. Mary was probably right about this, but the thought of Anne-Margaret leaving him was unbearable.

"She is my family, Mary. What will I do without her?"

"Good heavens, Thomas, you do have a tendency for the dramatic. She's not dying; she's just seeing what life has to offer outside of Sydney. Think of the experiences she could have, the people she'll meet. Don't deny her the opportunity to find her own way."

Thomas continued staring out the window. Mary had a spectacular view of the harbor here. This was her third house in Sydney, and she had decided that it was the one she'd die in. She had settled in Vaecleuse, a relatively new area, a bit out of town, but the views looking back into the harbor were breathtaking. On a clear day, you could see almost to Parrametta and beyond. He had thought about relocating out here, but it was so far from the shop, and the house in Woolloomooloo had become home for him and Anne-Margaret.

"Supposing I agreed that she should attend university somewhere else, and I'm not saying she should, mind you. But if I were, where were you thinking?"

Well, at least he might be somewhat open to the idea, thought Mary. "What about San Francisco?"

"Are you mad?" he quickly turned to face her. "San Francisco is a six-week trip, and a rough one at that. What would she find in San Francisco that she couldn't find here or in London?"

"It's such a lively city, Thomas. London is so dreary. San Francisco is growing, it's vibrant. It has wonderful museums and cultural attractions. It has new universities, and it's a breathtakingly beautiful place. You know some people even say it's a bit like Sydney. It's on the water, built on hills. When I was there last year, I positively fell in love with the place."

"You've already decided all this, haven't you?" Thomas said as he narrowed his eyes. "You've probably already gotten her admitted and found her a place to live."

"Well, I hadn't gotten that far, but yes, I have given it some thought."

"Have you spoken to Anne-Margaret about it?" With this he stared right at her. He knew he could tell if she was telling the truth or not if he was looking right into her eyes.

"Well, I have asked her about what her plans are for university. She said she supposed she would attend here."

Thomas raised his eyebrows.

"Really? That's the only discussion you've had with her about it?" Thomas knew she wasn't being completely honest with him.

"Well, I might have shared with her some of my stories from my last trip to San Francisco."

"Uh-huh. That's what I thought." He turned to gaze out the window again.

After a pause of several minutes he turned back to her.

"Do you think she wants to leave Sydney?"

Mary was pained to have to answer this. The last thing she wanted to do was to hurt Thomas's feelings. She knew of no one who had raised a finer child and completely on his own. She was afraid he might feel as though Anne-Margaret no longer needed him. But after thinking a moment, she decided that Thomas's feelings were not as important as Anne-Margaret's future.

"I do, " she said softly.

"I don't suppose you'll need to bring these along with you to San Francisco?" Thomas inquired as he held up Anne-Margaret's woodworking tools. He had given them to her for her twelfth birthday.

"I hope not. Otherwise, you'll be paying a lot of money for me to be making furniture. I think we should leave those here, so I'll have them when I come back."

It was the first mention of coming back that she had uttered to him, and they both realized it at the same time.

"Will you be back?" he said.

"Papa," she said, taking his hand, "home is always where you come back to."

Anne-Margaret had been accepted to all three universities she had applied to, passing her entrance exams easily, and she was enthusiastically looking forward to going away. Although she knew she would miss her father terribly, she was thrilled to be leaving Sydney and going somewhere new. Thomas had taken her to London when she was a baby to meet her grandparents, but she had no recollection of the trip, and they never made another one. Anne-Margaret concluded that his seeing her mother's family in the place where they had fallen in love and married was just too painful for her father. Her grandparents had been to Sydney twice since that first trip. But with that exception, the furthest she had traveled was to Victoria with her father when he was working on designs for Parliament House. Mary Tilden had shown her photographs of San Francisco, and Anne-Margaret was breathless.

Mary would accompany them on the trip. Anne-Margaret had asked her to, and Mary thought it would be a good opportunity to visit her sister, who had recently moved to San Francisco. So with steamer trunks packed to capacity and a few pieces of furniture, the three set out for San Francisco in late July of 1902.

Margaret would be attending the San Francisco College for Women, which had opened just three years earlier. It was a Catholic university, which Thomas didn't really care for, but the liberal arts education Anne-Margaret would receive there was already becoming quite highly regarded.

The night before they were to board the ship, as they waited for porters to come and collect their belongings for the next day, Thomas sat down with Anne-Margaret in the parlor. They seldom used this room—it seemed so formal. It was more common for them to be in Thomas's study or the parlor off the kitchen, but Thomas had a reason for this room. It had been Margaret's favorite room. The high windows let in an abundance of light and each piece of furniture had been designed and crafted by Thomas. Many of the pieces had actually been Margaret's creations, her drawings that Thomas then crafted. He made modifications here and there, but for the most part, they were of Margaret's vision, and many of those pieces were re-created for other homes in Sydney.

This was where Thomas moved the dressing mirror after Margaret died. He couldn't bear to look at it each morning in their bedroom, and yet he still wanted to feel its presence. Sometimes at night, the shadows of light in the parlor created reflections that he swore looked just like her. He knew he was partially dreaming, but it was the only place where he still really felt her presence.

Thomas was seated on a settee, Anne-Margaret on an overstuffed ottoman in front of him.

"Anne-Margaret, there is something I want you take with you to San Francisco. It belonged to your mother, and I know she would want you to have it."

"To Mother?"

Anne-Margaret sat, waiting for Thomas to present her with a small box containing a piece of her jewelry. Thomas had always given Anne-Margaret a piece of her mother's jewelry on special occasions.

Thomas rose from the settee and walked to the mirror.

"I gave this mirror to your mother as a wedding gift. I never saw her look lovelier than when she was looking at her reflection in it. I want you to take it with you, to connect you to this place, to me, to your mother."

He added thoughtfully, "I've always thought that the mirror's reflection could show you your soul. At least it always seemed to show your mother's."

Anne-Margaret was so touched, she was speechless. Her father had told her the story of the mirror when she was twelve years old, and she knew how much it meant to him, and to her mother. She walked over to him and threw her arms around his neck.

"Oh, Papa, thank you. I can't think of another thing you could give me that would mean home to me more than this mirror. Every time I look into the glass, I will see your reflection in it."

The journey to San Francisco was arduous and long. Crossing the Pacific was treacherous, and two bouts of bad weather had most of the passengers seasick and weary. But about four days out of San Francisco, the weather turned glorious, and the prospect of being so close to the end of the journey, combined with good weather buoyed everyone's spirits. The last night at sea was quite an event, with Thomas, Anne-Margaret, and Mary seated at the captain's table. Also seated at the table was a young man from Melbourne who was headed to Stanford University in Palo Alto. Anne-Margaret felt as though she already had met one kindred spirit.

The view from the entrance of the harbor at Sydney was breathtaking, and having seen it several times, Thomas prepared himself for a similar vista as the ship rounded the last bend below Baker Beach and moved into the mouth of the San Francisco Bay. The water became quite rough for a few moments, as three currents converged at the opening of the bay, but soon, the water calmed and most of the passengers had found a spot somewhere on the railing to view their arrival.

The view of the city was breathtaking, and the views of the east to Oakland and north to Marin were like nothing Thomas had seen. The ferries traveled back and forth between several points on the bay, shuttling passengers to and fro, just as the Sydney ferries did. But the landscape, although similar to Sydney's, had its own distinct appearance. The vegetation was a different tone of green, the sky a different shade of blue. It was as if the city had made sure there was no other place like it on earth. Mary pointed out the spectacular mansions on Nob Hill, quite visible from the ship's deck. Crocker, Huntington, Stanford, Flood, and Hopkins had built the grandest palaces that Thomas had ever seen. He could only imagine the furnishings inside. What would Mr. William Morris have had to say about that?

He watched Anne-Margaret's face as she took it all in, and although the dull ache of knowing he would be making the return journey alone was beginning to set in, he knew as he looked at her that this was the right decision. He thought at that very moment, she had never looked more like her mother. She had the exact same look on her face right now that Margaret had worn when they sailed into Sydney. Anticipation, anxiety, hope, fear, all a jumble between forehead and chin.

As they pulled into the dock just beyond the ferry building, Thomas felt amazingly at peace about bringing Anne-Margaret here. During the entire voyage, he had been slightly irritable, not sleeping well, eating sporadically, but the minute he saw the city, he somehow quieted. As he watched her now, he realized he had never seen her so full of life, so full of enthusiasm. She had an adventurous spirit, and this was the right place for her now.

Mary had arranged for them to stay at her sister's while Anne-Margaret would be settling in to her new living arrangements. She had been assigned to a small women's rooming house, a dormitory really, requiring a short walk or trolley ride to the campus. It housed twelve young women, all students at the San Francisco College for Women. Each room shared a bath with one other room, and Anne-Margaret's "bath mate" was a young woman from Marin County. She would be living in the rooming house during the week, and most likely returning to Marin County on the weekends. Her name was Kathryn Porter, and she was enthralled to meet her bath mate, who she knew came from Australia. Australia! She wondered if she came from a sheep station in the outback or her father was some character like Ned Kelly. It all sounded so adventurous. Upon meeting Anne-Margaret, she knew right away she was not in fact from a sheep station and her father was not an outlaw, but nevertheless, the two young women became fast friends.

The room was small, and Anne-Margaret lamented over where to place the mirror. After having Kathryn help her move it three times, she settled on a spot toward the end of her bed, at an angle so that the light from the window would keep it illuminated. She quickly noticed that as the light moved across the horizon, the mirror took on a different tone. Kathryn was somewhat enthralled with the fact that it was a free-standing mirror and pivoted it back and forth, checking her reflection as the mirror moved back and forth. Anne-Margaret didn't share with her the history of the mirror, other than to say that her father had given it to her mother as a wedding gift.

Mary Tilden and Anne-Margaret spent the next several days making sure Anne-Margaret was properly outfitted for school. Thomas accompanied them on some of these journeys, but mostly he was content to walk the streets of the city, exploring the different neighborhoods, particularly around the area where Anne-Margaret would be. He wanted to make sure he had a clear picture in his mind of the places that Anne-Margaret would later describe to him. It would make it easier for him to visualize what her life was like there.

After almost four weeks in San Francisco, the time came to say good-bye. Anne-Margaret was to begin class on Tuesday, and Thomas and Mary were scheduled to sail for Sydney the Saturday before. Both Thomas and Anne-Margaret sobbed as they said their good-byes at the dock, realizing it would be a long time before they were to see one another again. They spoke of the Christmas holidays, but neither of them thought they would travel. Crossing the Pacific that time of year was treacherous at best. So it was with a heavy heart that Thomas boarded, propped up by Mary Tilden, saddened by the thought that the girl he had seen every day of her life since the day she was born would be only a reflection in his mind, probably for several years.

Kathryn had accompanied Anne-Margaret to the dock to see her father off and was planning on loading her immediately onto the ferry with her for Marin. A weekend in the country would be a pleasant distraction and would give her time to recover before Tuesday classes.

Anne-Margaret stood on the dock until the horns sounded, and waved to her father and Mary, who had made their way to a spot along the railing. She stood waving until they were long out of sight.

"Miss Anne-Margaret, we have a very important lunch appointment. I think we should go, don't you?" Kathryn turned and said to her.

Anne-Margaret dried her cheeks, used her hankie to blow her nose, and turned to Kathryn.

"Yes, I do. I'm done with all this sniveling."

Anne-Margaret loved college life. She loved everything about it. She loved being challenged by her professors; she loved the passion of education and learning. She also was quite enjoying being one of a handful of women attending college at that time. Because the San Francisco College for Women was a Catholic university, it was affiliated with the University of San Francisco, a Jesuit college for men. In fact, some class offerings were offered through USF, and Anne-Margaret participated in several. Although some men were put off by her forwardness, especially when sharing her opinions in class, several liked her challenging personality.

Most weekends, Anne-Margaret accompanied Kathryn to Marin County, where they rode horses, swam in the pond, and read or studied. Some weekends, when Anne-Margaret was particularly busy with papers or exams, she would stay behind. It was those weekends that she ached for her father and for home. She wrote him a letter each week, as did he to her, but with their delivery coming across open ocean on ships, sometimes she would receive four or five at once. She loved reading them at night before she went to bed. He told of all that was going on at home, including what appeared to her a deepening relationship with Mary Tilden, which pleased Anne-Margaret tremendously. She always thought it odd that her father had never remarried, and now that Anne-Margaret was no longer his paramount concern, maybe it was time. She hoped so.

She wrote of her classes, her friends, her weekends

in Marin County with Kathryn, and of a growing interest in literature. Anne-Margaret had always been a voracious reader, so to be studying literature and its interpretation was fascinating to her. She was seeing a few young men socially, but no one in particular that was serious, she assured her father. Some of the men found her intimidating because she was so outspoken and direct. She wanted someone who was interested in her ideas and wanted to hear what she thought about things. She had seen the young man she had met aboard the ship who was attending Stanford University just once. He had come to San Francisco to take part in some sort of academic competition with men from USF, and they arranged to meet. But he was not as she remembered him. In fact, she thought him quite pompous and downright uninteresting. No, she wrote her father, no chance of her being married off anytime soon.

The mirror witnessed every event in Anne-Margaret's life, as it had for her mother. The elation of having a paper published in a scholarly journal, the despair of unrequited love for one of her professors, the profound loss of Kathryn's mother, who had become a dear friend, after a long illness. Her father had been right about the mirror reflecting the soul. Nothing could be hidden from it. As the mirror watched in earnest, Anne-Margaret took it all in. She learned more about dealing with emotional setbacks in the three years at school than she had in the previous twenty.

Her father had never been one to talk about his feelings, and Anne-Margaret arrived as a teenager somewhat unprepared for adulthood. But her experiences here had changed all of that. As she stood in front of the mirror, she thought about how much of her growing up it had witnessed and how precious the time here had been. What would her mother have though of all this? How she wished she had known her.

Anne-Margaret continued to focus her studies on literature, and when she neared graduation, she told her father she wanted to stay one more year to complete work for her master's degree through a joint program offered at USF. She was to be one of only two women admitted to the program. Although her father was heartbroken at the prospect of her staying another year, he knew it was what she wanted. Although he and Mary Tilden had married by this time and had visited Anne-Margaret twice since she had come to San Francisco, he longed for the "everydayness" of her. The idea of another year seemed torturous. He tried to convince her to come back and complete her work in Australia, but she would have none of it.

"It's not really even a whole year, Papa. I'll be home just as fall starts there," she said in her last letter.

While he didn't embrace the idea, he was thrilled that she wanted to come back home when she finished. He had never really gotten over the fear that she would never be back at all as he left her at the dock four years before. He truly believed that she would never call Sydney home again after four years in San Francisco, and had any of the young men she saw socially ever really impressed her, she wouldn't have. Thomas considered himself fortunate that she was so discriminating when it came to men.

Kathryn finished college in the spring of 1905 and headed back to Marin, but only temporarily. She was to be married in the summer, and Anne-Margaret was thrilled for her. She was marrying a young man who was from a very prominent San Francisco family and who had attended the University of San Francisco. Although Anne-Margaret knew she would miss Kathryn terribly that last year, she was overjoyed to have her in San Francisco, where she could still see her on a regular basis. The woman who moved in to replace her was a first-year, and Anne-Margaret was polite and pleasant to her, but the two never became the friends that she and Kathryn did.

The fall and winter came and went quickly, and before Anne-Margaret knew it, she had finished the advanced degree program and was preparing to return to Sydney. Two of her professors had asked her to stay on as a graduate teaching assistant, but she said no. She wanted to ensure that the experience she had had could be brought to women in Australia. She had her heart set on teaching literature at the University of Sydney, which had started to admit women just the year before. She was certain there were no women faculty members, and Anne-Margaret saw no reason to not be the first.

She packed all of her belongings except for the things she would need for her journey. She would be sailing with only personal items; her furniture and other larger items were to be shipped later. She was anxious to get home, and the ship that was sailing first could only accommodate passengers and light freight, mostly refrigerated meats, vegetables, and fruits, heading back to Sydney. So her heavier items would sail behind her and would arrive in Sydney about a month after she did. This bothered her only when it came to the mirror. The mirror had never been out of her family's possession since her father had made it. She felt as though she was sending her own child on its own. She also worried about damage and loss, or worse, theft, but she didn't have the patience to wait another month. She wanted to be home. It was a decision that would haunt her the rest of her life.

On the morning of April 14, 1906, Anne-Margaret Smyth sailed for Sydney. It was an unusually warm spring day, quite humid for San Francisco and very still. Good weather for traveling on open ocean. Kathryn and her husband had come to see her off. They had also taken on the task of seeing that her large items were on the next ship out, sometime later that month. She tearfully hugged Kathryn good-bye, with promises from both to visit, although Anne-Margaret did not think Kathryn would ever come to Sydney. She was pregnant with her first child, and Anne-Margaret presumed that she would never leave San Francisco. She stood on the railing all the way out past the opening at the mouth of the bay. And as the ship started to change its heading to the South, she turned back for one last glance at the city she had come to love.

Four days later, at just after 5:00 A.M., it would be changed forever.

A great curiosity must be both a great gift and a weighty burden. What must drive a person to search for an answer to one of life's questions? Is it the desire to be right, or the desire to just know? I do not know her yet; she is still a mystery to me. But she is complicated and passionate and I am drawn to her for some reason. She is different than those who have come before. She does not know peace, I think. Every moment is spent in search of something.

What is it that she is searching for?

Beth—2002

As Beth drove up Sir Francis Drake Boulevard, she worried that this was a bad idea. Mr. Allen had said his mother would be of no help to her. So why was she here on a Saturday morning, winding her way through Kentfield? She pulled into the parking area and made her way to the front entrance. A young woman was sitting, reading some trashy romance novel with Fabio on the front cover.

"May I help you?" she asked, clearly irritated to be disturbed from her Pulitzer Prize–winning novel.

"I'm here to see Nan Allen, please."

"I need you to sign in. Leave your car keys here please."

Beth's look must have given the question away.

"We've had residents lift them out of purses and pockets. Had one guy that got all the way to Sausalito." She shook her head slowly, "They can't remember what time breakfast is, but they can lift a set of keys, know which car they go to, and get all the way to Sausalito. Strange disease, wouldn't you say?"

Beth dropped her keys into the desk drawer and watched as the woman locked the drawer.

"Just stop by here on your way out. Follow me."

Beth followed her down the long hallway toward a set of double doors at the end. Before reaching the doors, Beth noticed two other corridors to her left and right, with an open entryway. No locked doors.

"These doors stay open?"

"Yes. Those wings are for assisted living residents. They have all their marbles. Just need a little help with dressing or getting to the dining hall. We don't worry about them getting disoriented or injured."

She reached the double doors and coded in an access number, and the doors swung back. The hallway was eerily quiet. No one seemed to be there.

"Mrs. Allen is in Room 104, second door on the right. Would you like me to call someone to go in with you?"

"Is she dangerous?" Beth was having visions of sitting across an empty table with a giant armed guard at one end.

"Oh, no. Some folks just feel more comfortable if there is someone else in the room."

"I'll be fine. Thank you."

"When you're ready to leave, just ask one of the nurses at the station to code you out." She lifted her head toward a large central desk area down the hallway, about halfway, to indicate where it was.

The woman turned and disappeared through the double doors. When they sealed closed with an enormous sucking sound, Beth contemplated turning around and forgetting the whole thing. She had to admit she was intimidated by the surroundings, and Beth didn't intimidate easily. She stood in the hallway a moment and thought to herself sadly, *What a way to end a life.*

She made her way to 104 and knocked as she was opening the door.

"Mrs. Allen?"

"Yes? Is that you, Patricia?"

As Beth walked into the room, she saw her. A

diminutive woman, very nicely dressed, her white hair pulled back in a perfect chignon. She looked as though she might be off to a ladies lunch. Beth was expecting someone who stared rather vacantly, but from all outward appearances, Nan Allen seemed quite alert and interested in her visitor.

"No, it's not Patricia. My name is Beth Graham. I spoke with your son about coming to see you."

"Patricia always brings me cookies."

Hmmm, thought Beth, *no cookies*.

"I have a mint. Would you like a mint?"

"No, thank you. I'd like a cookie."

Now what? thought Beth. If she were going to get her to talk, she'd have to have something to warm her up.

"I also have a chocolate bar. How about that?"

Her faced beamed.

"I love chocolate. But they don't like me to have it."

"Well, it will be our little secret." Beth hoped it wouldn't send her into a diabetic coma. Why wouldn't they want her to have it?

She smiled sweetly and held out her hand. Beth noticed she still wore her wedding band on her left hand. Her hands were quite delicate, the skin wrinkly, but a beautiful tone. As she looked at her face, she noticed her skin tone was beautiful everywhere. *Blessed with a good complexion, I guess*, thought Beth.

Beth pulled up the guest chair and sat in front of her and asked her a few small-talk questions. Nothing too taxing, and Nan Allen appeared lucid and pleasant, so Beth ventured on.

"Mrs. Allen, can you tell me about your friend, Dorothea Renton?"

"Thea, of course. Thea was a dear friend. We met when we were single, career girls. All of us were career girls when the war was on."

"Really? What was she like?"

"She liked to drink Manhattans." She nibbled at the chocolate bar. As she broke off each piece, she was slow and deliberate, as though she was trying to make that candy last all afternoon.

"Manhattans?"

"Yes. She said it was what all great writers liked to drink."

"You knew her when she was a writer?"

"I knew her when she wrote for the paper. And later, when she wrote books. I never really cared for her books, you know."

"I've only read one, so I don't really have an opinion. You mentioned the paper?"

"She worked at the *Chronicle*. City desk."

"Did you work at the *Chronicle* also?"

"Oh, no. I worked at the City of Paris—special events."

"Really. That sounds wonderful." At this point, Beth began to wonder if what she was hearing was true, but she saw no reason to not spend a few more minutes. Beth guessed that Robert Allen didn't visit his mother much, and Mrs. Allen probably spent a good bit of time alone. It wouldn't be the worst thing to spend a morning with her and have her feel a little less lonely.

"Mrs. Allen, I'm trying to find out about a mirror that was in Thea's house." The minute the words were out her mouth, she wished she hadn't said them. There was no way this woman was going to know or remember anything about that mirror.

"You were in Thea's house? Did you meet Jack? He's a wonderful man."

"No, I didn't. Was Jack her husband?"

"Oh, no. They were never married. Jack could tell you about the mirror."

"Does Jack have a last name?"

"Kennedy. You know, the president."

Beth's excitement over having possibly tripped upon something that might help her was quickly squelched, but she didn't want to agitate the woman, so she went along with it.

"Oh, yes. The president. Well, that must have been exciting. Did the mirror belong to him?"

"Of course not. It was McSchuyler's mirror."

"McSchuyler?"

"The man that owned the bar." Her tone indicated a slight frustration, as if Beth was supposed to already know who McSchuyler was.

Beth wanted to keep her on this train of thought, so she thought quickly.

"Oh, the bar where Thea would go for Manhattans?"

"Yes. But I never drank Manhattans. Only martinis. In 1945, everyone drank martinis. Except for Thea of course. She said all great writers drank Manhattans. Did you bring me any cookies?"

Beth suddenly realized she had probably gotten as much as she could from this visit. Nan Allen had turned away and was looking out the window.

"Well, thank you, Mrs. Allen. Next time we visit, I'll be sure to bring you some cookies." She patted the old woman's hand, and as she did, Nan Allen grasped it tightly.

Nan Allen stared at her vacantly. It was clear she had absolutely no idea what they had been discussing. Robert Allen had told her it would be a waste of time, and he was right. At least the drive over had been pleasant. And she was halfway to Stinson, so all was not lost.

As she reached the door, she turned to say one last good-bye, and Mrs. Allen stared right into her eyes.

"They came in the mirror, you know."

"Excuse me?"

"Both of Thea's great loves. They came in the mirror."

Beth had no idea what she was trying to tell her, but she didn't think it was crazy rambling. It was too purposeful, too clear.

As Beth started down the hallway to the nurse's station, she decided she'd had enough of this detective work. It was a lovely mirror. Period. She would have it refinished and leave it in the house as it stood. She didn't really need to know where it came from anyway.

Monday morning brought a cold, driving rain. Beth and Drew had stayed out at the beach and were driving back into the city on Monday morning. The traffic slowed up Waldo grade as the snake of the morning commute slowed to a crawl.

"So, you'll call the tree guys, and I'll call the tile man. Right? Beth?"

Beth continued to gaze straight ahead out the front window. She kept thinking about her conversation with Mrs. Allen. She had read that Alzheimer's patients got truth mixed up with fantasy, so that some parts of what they said were accurate and other parts were not. So what was true and what wasn't? If she could somehow figure that out, she might know where to dig.

"Beth? Still with me, baby?"

"Hmmm? Oh, yeah, I'll call the tree guy."

"Thought I'd lost you there for a minute. Did you want me to get a quote for fixing the broken tiles or for having the whole thing retiled?"

Beth thought for a moment.

"Get quotes for both, but I'm thinking we just get it regrouted and cleaned up for now. We can gut the whole thing later when we know what we want."

"Okay. And make sure you tell them that the trees just need to be thinned out. I don't want to lose the privacy over those back windows."

"Yes, dear."

Beth returned to her empty gaze as the windshield wipers began to mesmerize her.

Drew knew exactly where her mind was.

"Look, the old lady sounds totally daffy. Give it a rest, will you? We know the mirror is English antique, and it's lovely. Can't you be happy with that?"

"I'm not unhappy. I'm just curious, I guess. Aren't you? I thought lawyers were supposed to have great intellectual curiosity."

"I must have been sick the day they taught that at law school," he said, smiling.

Beth sighed, "Part of what she said is complete nonsense. President Kennedy? Not likely. In 1945 he was about twenty years old. But it will be easy to find out if Dorothea Renton worked at the *Chron*, right? And it should be easy to track down a McSchuyler's bar, right? So some of it could be true, mixed up with some stuff that's fantasy."

Drew rolled his eyes.

"Okay, suppose those parts are accurate. Then what? There probably isn't anyone alive with mental capacity intact that could tell you about that mirror."

"It's like a puzzle, Drew. One piece links to another. And at some point, if I can't find a piece that fits, then I'm done." She squeezed his arm and looked right at him. "I just can't help but think that the mirror has a story to tell. Maybe many stories. I don't know."

"Uh-huh. Done. We'll see about that. It has been my experience that when you get started on something, you are like a dog with a slipper. You will not be satisfied until it is completely ripped to shreds."

The traffic began to pick up a little speed over the bridge and along Doyle Drive. Beth glanced at her watch. Seven forty-five. She had a meeting at 8:30. If the traffic kept moving, she would have plenty of time to get Kim started on her little research project.

Beth quickly took an interest in their route.

"No, don't take Beach. It always backs up at Columbus. Go up the hill and take Bush, all the lights are timed in to downtown."

"Ah, glad to see you're back. I didn't think you were paying attention." He headed up the hill into Pacific Heights and turned left onto Bush Street. Beth took another glance at her watch. Seven-fifty. Perfect.

Beth flew into her office, grabbed coffee, and yelled for Kim.

"Yes, your majesty? You rang?" Kim stood in Beth's doorway with her usual droll, disinterested look.

Beth had been crafting this conversation in the car with Drew and had come up with the perfect scheme.

"You know how you've been saying you're getting

tired of administrative duties?"

"Is this a trick question?"

Beth smiled.

"No. It's just that I've been thinking that maybe you might be a candidate for a research assistant for Dan or Bill."

"I don't have a college degree. We've been through this."

"I know that. Here's my plan: you work on a project for me, and if it goes well, I'll recommend you to Dan and Bill. With Mr. Three Last Names headed back to business school, they are going to have to find a replacement. You're great at finding stuff on the web, you'll call anyone, and you're good at following your instincts. Besides, I need this project done anyway, and I'm not asking Mr. Three Last Names to work on it." She paused briefly before adding, "It's not billable time."

"Oh, I see. The glorified errand girl again."

"This is real research. I'm the client."

"Well, producing power point presentations is really fulfilling you know. But I suppose I can help you out." She cracked a smile. "Do you really think Dan and Bill would consider me?"

"You have nothing to lose on this."

"Okay, I'm in."

"Okay. You know that mirror I told you about in the house we bought?"

"The one I called the appraiser on?"

"That's the one. The appraiser told me it was nineteenth-century English antique. Made for a royal, somehow got itself to the U.S. So I have a mirror that was made in the 1880s and ends up in a house at Stinson

Beach in 2002. I want to fill in the blanks."

"Has it occurred to you that anyone who might know anything about this mirror is dead?"

"That's what makes the research a challenge. I figure if you can help me piece this together, then you can research anything."

"You have anything else besides what the appraiser told you?"

"Don't laugh. I went to see an elderly woman who knew the owner of the house."

"Okay, that sounds promising. Did she know anything?"

Beth winced.

"She has Alzheimer's disease."

"Oh, great. Did she tell you she was actually Queen Victoria reincarnated and she brought the mirror over here by steamer ship?"

"Funny. Actually, she was quasi-lucid, which makes me think that part of her story may hang together. There were parts of it that were nonsense, like her saying that the woman who owned my house knew President Kennedy, but there were parts that could be plausible."

"Like what?" Kim sipped her coffee slowly and raised her eyebrows. Beth could tell her interests were piqued.

"Well, first, check to see if there was a Dorothea Renton that worked at the *Chron* in the 1940s. While you're at it, check on Nan Allen as well. She also mentioned a McSchuyler's bar or restaurant. When I asked her about the mirror, she said 'McSchuyler's mirror.' That part seemed a little flaky, but you never know."

"What else?"

"That's it. Except for the reference about President

Kennedy." Beth smirked slightly. "I'm guessing that's not worth chasing down."

"Okay. I've got a ton of work to do for Mr. Three Last Names today. He gave me a pile of work to do today for his trip tomorrow, and as usual, no one in the world can make a gray scale chart quite like I can." She thrust her index finger down her throat; the universal sign for "gag me."

"You know, if you'd just go out with him once, your misery would be over. He'd realize the two of you have no future, and you could both get back to work."

"I've thought of that, but not even I can stoop that low. I think I was already out of high school when he was born." She glanced at her watch. "You are officially two minutes late."

"Yeah, yeah, yeah. They'll wait. I have all the answers, remember?"

About 9:30 that night, the phone rang.

"It must be my mother. She has a knack for calling right after I've had the TV on for fifteen minutes and am now sucked into whatever it is I'm watching." Beth rolled off the sofa and into the kitchen to get the phone.

"Hello?"

"Dorothea Renton did work at the *Chronicle*, 1944 to 1949. She wrote copy for the city editor. She had a couple of bylines, a few front pages on some public works scandal in 1945, where the mayor was doing favors for his friends. No sign of Nan Allen though."

Well, Beth thought, *Nan Allen may not be completely without her marbles.* She closed her eyes, hoping the rest of her story might actually be true.

"And McSchuyler's?"

"Nothing. But I'm still looking. I was actually going to ask you if I could come in late tomorrow. I was thinking I might go the archive room at the *Chron* and see what I can dig up. You know, old photos, something."

"Okay with me. What about Mr. Three Last Names?"

"On his way to Minneapolis with perfect gray scale charts."

"Okay, I'll see you around lunchtime?"

"Righty-oh."

Beth rambled back into the den during the commercial break. Drew was reading a document of some sort, and she realized that whatever she had been watching wasn't all that interesting now, given she missed a good portion of the story line while she was on the phone.

"So, the lady wasn't as loony as you thought," Beth whispered.

"Oh? She really did know Jack Kennedy?" he replied, glancing over the top of his glasses.

"Well, I don't know about that, but Dorothea Renton did work at the *Chronicle* in the 1940s."

"Well, I'll be. Another piece to the mystery, Miss Drew? Will Bess and George be returning to the secret staircase for another clue?"

"Perhaps. Kim, aka Bess, will be giving me a recap in the morning."

"Excellent. Maybe I could interest the detective in another investigation?" He pushed aside his pile of reading and lay down on the sofa. Beth slowly lay down on top of him.

"I don't know. I'm pretty busy with the case I'm working on," she whispered into his ear as she moved her hands down his sides.

It was all Beth could do to not race into the office, but she knew Kim wouldn't be there until noon. She managed to keep herself occupied and cover for the missing Kim, the insistent Mr. Three Last Names calling twice from Minneapolis, until she arrived about 12:30.

"Where have you been?" Beth asked insistently.

"You're the one who told me to go! I thought you were training me for research!"

"I am, I am. I'm just—" Beth stammered as she drummed on her desk with a pencil.

"Impatient? Demanding? Oh, no, not you."

"Sorry." Beth waited for what she thought was an appropriate interval and then fired again. "Did you find anything? I've got Chinese here for you."

"Oh, thanks. I'm starving. All of that intellectual stimulation really works up an appetite."

Kim opened up the chow mein, painfully slowly, thought Beth, took a big chopstick full of noodles, and sat down.

"Well" she said, with a noodle sneaking out of her mouth, "the old lady isn't crazy."

"I knew it!"

"But she may have a problem with her enunciation. Either that or you have a problem with your hearing."

Beth looked at her quizzically.

"What does that mean?"

"It means that 'McSchuyler' is actually Max Schuyler." Beth's face broke into a broad smile as Kim dropped her chopsticks into the chow mein carton. "Don't look so smug. If you knew all of this already, you could have saved me a lot of time."

"No, I mean I knew there was something there. So I

butchered the name a little. Sue me."

"Schuyler's was sort of a *Chronicle* watering hole, right around the corner from the *Chron* on Front Street. I talked to a guy in the archive room who's a third-generation *Chron* employee. He said his granddad used to go to Schuyler's almost every night after they put the paper to press. Apparently a lot of folks from the mayor's office went there, too. They'd find out what was going to be in the morning edition the night before, and then be ready with a response by morning. Spin doctors, even back then."

"I've never heard of the place. Must not be around anymore."

"It's not. Went out of business in 1945. But," she said as she started another bite of noodles, "the archive boy knows someone who does know about it." Kim chewed painfully slowly. Every minute for Beth was torture.

"And that would be?" Beth replied sarcastically.

"Max Schuyler's great-grandson. He lives in Berkeley. I'm meeting him tomorrow night."

"Only you could turn a research project into a date. Meet him somewhere very public. He might be an axe murderer."

"I've had a lot of recent experience dating total strangers. I know the drill. I suggested Hawthorne Lane."

"Good choice."

"Yeah, well, the 'Director of Research' for Breyer-McSwain has certain standards to uphold."

"Oh, you are good."

Kim smiled.

"Pass me a fortune cookie. I'm feeling lucky."

Beth was on her third cup of coffee when Kim arrived for work the morning after her "date."

"Well? Well?"

Beth was frantically tapping on her desk with a pencil. Kim knew in an instant she was in caffeine overdrive.

"I thought we agreed that two cups was it for you in the morning."

"I've been waiting for you. I had to stay occupied."

"Working on something that's actually billable time is good for that, you know."

"Thanks for the tip. I guess the Director of Research has become quite a corporate ladder climber. C'mon, you are torturing me! Tell me, tell me, tell me!"

"Well, he's a lawyer, but he doesn't practice. He's actually a teaching professor at Boalt Hall and—"

"Not about that! About Max Schuyler!"

"Oh, that. Right." Kim was clearly distracted by her good fortune in meeting someone who wasn't gay or married.

"He said his great-granddad opened the bar shortly after the earthquake in 1906. He thought he remembered his dad telling him that some of the furniture was actually purchased out of reclamation from earthquake-damaged buildings. Sold it and all its contents in 1945, when he retired at sixty-five. He said it attracted a real San Francisco clientele during its heyday in the forties. The lunch crowd was mostly wheeler-dealers from the financial district, and the late-night crowd was from the paper and city hall."

"So, the mirror was probably in the bar, and she bought it when he closed it down?"

"Oh, the mirror was definitely in the bar." Kim

smiled, as though she was guarding a precious secret. She opened her bag and pulled out a plain manila envelope. Beth couldn't quite make out what was in it, until Kim opened it.

Photographs. Lots of them.

"Ben said his grandmother found them in his grandfather's things when he died. She didn't recognize a lot of them, but she thought she ought to keep them."

"Thank God for packrats."

Beth opened the folder and let the photos fall onto her desk. Kim picked up the one on top.

"See anything you recognize?"

It was an old tintype photo printed on paper that was so heavy, it was almost like cardboard. There was a man behind a bar, some other men on barstools, and there, in the background of the picture above the bar, in a horizontal orientation just as it was in her house, was the mirror.

I have the best seat in the house. From here, I see everything. I miss nothing. Those who enter, those who exit, those who stay longer than they should are all here. I have heard a thousand stories of good luck, ill will, happy homes, lost loves, broken souls, and that all-elusive meaning of life. I have watched more emotional range than I thought a human soul capable of delivering. But this is unusual. This soul is hard to unravel. Where is the crack in the foundation?

There always is one.

Dorothea—1945

Dorothea looked up at the clock anxiously. Seven-twenty. She told Nan she'd meet her at Schuyler's at seven. Pete Baker labored over her pages, back and forth. She couldn't tell what he was thinking, so she offered her thoughts.

"I say we run with it. What's the worst thing that could happen?" Thea wanted this story to run.

"Well, the mayor's office could make us look like asses for one thing. There isn't one quoted source in here. No one will go on the record. Everything is hearsay. 'Sources inside the mayor's office' sounds like the janitor." Pete Baker had been the city editor for over a decade. He'd been burned plenty and knew that cleaning up a story that wasn't ready wasn't worth it.

"Thea, I'll give you one more day—"

"No. Another day isn't going to change this story. No one is magically going to go on the record between seven twenty-five tonight and seven twenty-five tomorrow night."

"Well, then we wait until someone does. It's too risky. We can't afford to get the freeze-out from the mayor's office if this story is wrong. We need them."

"It's not wrong."

"I can't print it." He picked up the phone to the typesetting room and gave them orders. "Go with the story on the tree at the City of Paris as the lead."

"The Christmas tree at a department store? That's news?"

"It is today," he grumbled back.

Thea turned on her heels and walked out of his office. It was going to be a three-Manhattan night.

Nan waved at her from a side booth. Thea hung up her coat on the rack in the vestibule and snaked her way through the crowd to sit down. As she passed the bar, she saw another one of the copy editors.

"I told you he wouldn't run it," he said, never taking his eyes off of his drink.

"Thanks. Maybe next time you can tell me before I spend three days working on it."

"You're almost there. You need to find a source that will talk."

"Gee, that's a great idea. Maybe I'll take out a classified," she snarled back. She made her way through the crowded bar back to the table that Nan had secured.

"Well, you look like twelve miles of bad road. What happened? And why do you always run late when I'm here by myself?" Nan waved at the bartender as she was talking. "Martini and a Manhattan, Max." She looked at Thea again and quickly added, "Make the Manhattan stiff."

"Well, so much for my brilliant career. I can't get anything printed." Thea slumped into the booth.

"That's not true. Your story on the opera opening was fabulous."

"I don't want to cover opera openings and socialite weddings. I want to cover real news."

"What's so great about real news? It's all so depressing. Now that the war is over, I think you should write about fashion."

"You would."

"What's wrong with fashion? Women need guidance and counsel on fashion. You'd be providing a valuable service."

Max brought their drinks to the table.

"Special delivery." He glanced at Thea. "Tough day, dear?"

Thea practically drained the glass in one gulp and then looked up.

"Max, do you ever wonder how news gets made?"

"Nope. I know how it gets made. Some dumbass comes in here, has too many martinis, and shoots his mouth off about something he shouldn't."

"I can only hope for such a stroke of good fortune" Thea replied as she slugged down the last of her Manhattan. She looked at the empty glass and back at Max. "Guess I'll need another. I'll drink this one slow. I promise."

Thea was sitting facing the bar, watching the scene as Max did his best imitation from a roaring twenties movie. He'd survived two world wars from behind that bar. He'd also survived the earthquake in 1906 and, feeling himself fortunate, had opened the bar sometime after the earthquake with a lot of furniture and lighting that had actually survived the earthquake and the fires. It was an eclectic mix; some of the pieces actually had burn marks, or broken edges, every single piece had an amazing story behind it, and Max knew them all. The walls were lined with photographs of Max with interesting people. Several mayors, sports celebrities, movie stars, even a U.S. president or two.

She heard laughter and raised voices in the vestibule. Suddenly whatever Nan was talking about was not worth listening to. She had been her best friend for more than a decade, but on a day like today her "poor me" routine was grating on Thea.

Thea couldn't see what all the commotion was about in the vestibule, so she looked up over the bar and into the mirror. Thea had discovered this little trick from a guy at the paper. He had a reputation as a pit bull for getting a story, and if anyone saw him coming, they'd run the other way. So, he'd pick his mark in the mirror, undetected, and then pounce when he thought they looked amenable to talking, usually after a few drinks. From the angle she was seated, she had a perfect view of the entrance to the bar reflected in the mirror.

"I said, don't you think it would look better in the green? Thea? Are you listening to me?"

Suddenly Thea turned to face Nan.

"Green. Yes. Absolutely."

"You haven't heard a word I've said."

"I'm watching the commotion in the front."

Nan swiveled around.

"I can't see."

"I'll give you the details."

"You can't see either," Nan replied in an exasperated tone.

"I can see perfectly in the mirror over the bar. I'm at just the right angle." Nan realized that for as long as she had been coming here with Thea, she never really noticed the mirror. She knew it was there, but she didn't ever pause to reflect in it. As a rule, Nan didn't like mirrors. Too much reality. But she looked now and realized it was lovely. Quite old, she guessed. She knew Max had pieces that had survived the fires in 1906 and she wondered if this might be one of them. Her solitude was broken by the voices of three men entering the bar. Thea continued to watch the mirror intently and realized that she recognized two of them from the mayor's office. But the third was no one she had seen before. She would have remembered him. Tall, dark, and handsome. No, definitely not someone she knew.

Suddenly, he looked up in the mirror and caught her staring. She looked away quickly and pretended to be fascinated by whatever it was that Nan was talking about. But while keeping her head straightforward at Nan, her eyes were in the mirror. He cocked his head slightly and smiled at her—at least, she thought so—and sat down at the bar.

Well, she thought, *might be time for another round*.

"I'm going for another round. Want one?" Thea asked Nan.

"Okay, one more, but then I have to go. I have an early day tomorrow."

"New spring line to be displayed? When are you going to quit goofing around and get a real job?" Thea shot back as she slid out of the booth.

"When my father figures out he's still paying my allowance and decides to stop."

"Some people are born lucky."

"No, some people are born with trust funds." She giggled into the last of her martini glass.

Thea made her way up to the bar, which had gotten more crowded since she arrived. In addition to the usual crowd from the city room at the *Chron* and the politicos, there were a few new faces. One was the man Thea had been watching in the mirror.

"I thought you guys from City Hall didn't like to mix with the unwashed from the press," she said to the guy sitting with the handsome stranger.

"Ah, the lovely Thea. Still waiting to bust open a major crime ring in the mayor's office?" Ted Riddle was one of the press liaisons that she knew from the mayor's office. She thought he was a total creep, but she wanted to find out who his friend was.

"Well, it wouldn't be difficult. No such thing as a clean politician, you know." She leaned over to the tall, dark, and handsome friend and said, "I don't know if I would be seen with this guy. He's just waiting to be on the front page of the paper having been caught doing something really scandalous."

"I'll keep that in mind." His voice was deep and matched the rest of him.

"A really good scandal would make Tom like me even more, right?" Ted turned to his friend and laughed.

"A really good scandal would make you more interesting, true."

"Thea, meet my friend Tom Fallon. He's a lawyer. You two probably have nothing in common. Tom, this is my nemesis, Dorothea Renton."

"Your nemesis? You flatter me, Ted. I never knew you cared." She was speaking to Ted, but her eyes never left Tom Fallon's face. Nor did his eyes leave her. "What kind of law, Tom?"

"I'm a litigator. Mostly for construction companies and civil engineering firms that get sued when their buildings collapse, that sort of thing. Very noble, huh?" He took a swig of his drink. "And you must write for the paper that Ted speaks so highly of." He smiled as he brought his glass to his mouth and took the last swallow from his drink. Manhattan, Thea was guessing from the color.

"Yes, Ted's life makes my life possible. Every newspaper needs a couple of good buffoons in the mayor's office. Ted is perfect for the job."

Tom laughed out loud.

"Well, you've got the right guy for the job then," he said, grinning at Thea.

Thea remembered Nan coaching her to always leave them wanting more, so she grabbed the two drinks and spun around.

"Nice to meet you, Tom. My friend is probably getting thirsty." She looked over at Nan who was waving and signaling at her watch.

"Maybe I'll see you again some time," he said.

"Well, Ted can tell you, I'm here pretty often. You'd be amazed what you overhear in here." She shot a look at Ted as if to say she was watching him, but he had no idea what she was thinking. Tom did however.

She went back to Schuyler's every night that week and never took her eyes off the mirror, hoping he'd walk through the door. But he did not reappear.

The more Thea asked questions, the more she knew something was going on in the mayor's office with the public works projects. She called Ted and asked him for a list of all the contractors who had bid on the Western Addition project.

"Thea, c'mon. You know I can't give you that. The bids are all sealed."

"I don't care about bid amounts. I just want to see who's bidding."

"Well, that's public record. Go to the planning commission office, and they'll show you the bid list."

"So helpful today. Got a new girl?"

"You know I'm still waiting for you."

"Does the term 'when hell freezes over' mean anything to you?"

"No."

She laughed.

"You're not my type."

"What is your type?"

"Well, since you asked, I liked your friend Tom the other night." She winced the minute she said it. Now that Ted knew, she wouldn't get a moment's peace.

"Well, isn't that a coincidence? He asked about you as well."

Her heart leapt out of her chest.

"Well, maybe you can bring him to Schuyler's again sometime."

"Why don't I just tell him to call you? That would seem a little more direct and to the point, don't you think?"

"I'd like that. And thanks for the bid information."

"You won't find anything, Thea. It's clean."

"Did I say anything to imply it wasn't?"

"No, but I know you. You're always digging for dirt. There isn't any here."

"Meaning I should be digging elsewhere?"

"You know our friend Tom is actually doing some legal work for the city right now. Why don't you ask him what he's working on?"

"Meaning?"

"You're the reporter, Thea." The line went dead.

When the phone rang at her desk, she had just finished arguing with the copy editor about the use of who and whom.

She picked it up and jabbed.

"I have a master's degree in linguistics for Christ's sake. I'm pretty sure I know the proper usage of who and whom!"

"Okay, okay, I'm sure you do!" The voice did not belong to the copy editor. She froze when she recognized the voice, immediately, and her heart leapt in her chest.

"Oh, I'm so sorry. I thought you were someone else," she said trying to regain her composure.

"Clearly."

"Who is speaking, please?" she said in her most professional voice, although she knew exactly who it was.

"This is Tom Fallon. We met the other night at Schuyler's?"

"I remember you."

"Ted mentioned that it was okay with you if I called, so I'm calling." Okay, that was the stupidest thing he had ever said to a woman on the phone. What the hell was wrong with him?

"I'm glad you did. Call, I mean." What was she thinking? She was acting like a thirteen-year-old with her first crush.

"So what exactly is the proper usage of who and whom anyway? I always get that confused."

"Are you making fun of me?" She loved a sense of humor. She could always put a bag over their heads if she had to, but if they couldn't make her laugh, there was no point.

"No, just making small talk, stalling really. I was

wondering if you'd like to have dinner with me, maybe one night this week?"

"Yes, I'd like that very much. I'm free any night but Thursday."

"Then how about Thursday?" he asked.

"Thursday it is." She hung up the phone and softly sighed.

"So Ted tells me you're working for the city right now? What's that all about?" They met at Schuyler's after she closed out for the night at the paper. Thursday was her night for final proofs with the typesetter, so they didn't meet until around 8:30.

"I'm assisting with the review process for contracted bids. Providing information about the bidders building records, permits, hiring practices, that sort of thing. Fascinating, don't you think?" He rolled his eyes.

"Do I detect a note of sarcasm?" Thea quipped back.

"It was my turn in the pro bono pool. My firm does a lot of work for the city on a pro bono basis, and all the associates take a turn when they are in between cases. It was my turn."

"So I gather you're not thrilled with this assignment?"

"I'm a litigator, a good one. Pushing contracts around from one desk to another, reviewing documents that have been filed with the city or the state isn't what gets me going in the morning."

"Well, maybe you'll find something really interesting, like one of the bidders is a relative of the mayor and even though his firm isn't exactly top notch, the city awards him the bid anyway." She was trying to chew her meat daintily, but was having a tough time of it. When she looked up at Tom, he had his fork down and was pushing back from the table.

"What? What is it?" Dorothea could not imagine what had precipitated this reaction.

"Is that why you're having dinner with me? To dig up a story?"

"*No!*"

"Are you sure about that?"

"Yes. I told Ted I was interested in you before I knew what you were working on. I'm just naturally curious. I didn't mean to offend you or imply anything."

He pushed his chair back to the table and resumed eating. They both sat in silence for a while, and finally, Tom spoke up.

"Look, I like you Thea. But I don't want to end up in a news story."

"Why would you end up in a news story?"

"Isn't that what you do? Make news?"

"I don't make the news. I write about the news. My interest in you has nothing to do with the news. I'm sorry if I made you jumpy. I just wanted to find out more about what you did."

"I'm sorry, too. Overly sensitive."

Thea put her hands in her lap and looked directly across the table.

"I have no agenda here other than getting to know you better. Honest."

She glanced up at the bar and saw their reflection in the mirror. She decided she liked the way they looked together.

"What are you looking over my shoulder at?" He turned as he was saying it to see what she might be finding more interesting. He couldn't stand women who were constantly scanning the horizon for something better.

She waved at him in the mirror.
"Do you see it?"
"See what?"
"Our reflection."
He waved back.
"Looks good," he said, taking her hand.
"That's just what I was thinking."

They met most every night at Schuyler's from that evening on and it became their custom to wave in the mirror. The first of them already seated in their booth, the other arriving later.

She never asked him about his work in the mayor's office again, but she had not given up her quest for a story there, even after the city editor told her to quit looking for trouble. She concentrated on other city happenings, new building openings, local celebrities, and her favorite story on a group of earthquake survivors who met at the Ferry Building at 5:13 A.M. every April eighteenth.

But she kept digging in her spare time, pushing her contacts at City Hall, until one day over a burger with Ted Riddle, he said something that unnerved her.

"Tom should be heading back to his real job soon. It's a good thing—he's too good of a guy to get mixed up in all this."

"All what?"

Ted realized what he'd said and then also remembered Thea's line of work.

"All the City Hall stuff, politics, you know." He nervously took another bite of his lunch, trying to recover.

Thea didn't want Ted to know she was suspicious, so she changed the subject.

"I don't think he's interested in running for anything."

"Well, that's a relief."

"You don't think he'd make a good public servant?" she said sarcastically.

"Too honest."

Thea laughed, hoping that Ted would think that she'd missed the bait he'd thrown. But she didn't, and he knew it.

"Hey, you know, I finally tracked down the bid list for the WA project. The planning commission was very helpful, and I wanted to thank you for the help," she said between bites.

"Find anything interesting?"

"No, not really. The usual suspects. Wouldn't want to marry into their families, but not doing anything illegal either."

They finished their lunch and walked out into the sunlight. Thea prepared to go back downtown to the *Chron*, and Ted to City Hall.

"Hey, I shouldn't have said anything about Tom. Don't tell him, okay?" Ted kicked the ground with his shoe as he spoke.

"Not to worry. I have no idea what you are talking about." Thea smiled, gave Ted a peck on the cheek and said, "Thanks for lunch."

She turned on her heels and headed purposefully back to her office. She was going to go over that list again with a more critical eye. There was something there. She could tell by Ted's reaction when she mentioned it.

Tom had stopped talking about work to the point where Dorothea was becoming a little worried. She knew he was scheduled to conclude his pro bono work for the city and return to litigation, and she found herself looking forward to it. She was sure he would be less preoccupied.

"You're awfully quiet tonight." Thea looked at him, hoping to see if his expression changed.

"Sorry. Just tired I guess. I'll be finished on Friday at City Hall, so I'm trying to get all the loose ends tied up."

"You don't strike me as the type for loose ends."

"All the more reason to have them tied up then, don't you think?" he snapped back.

"Tom, I don't know what is bothering you, but I'm going to go on home. Why don't you call me next week when you're back in your office and we can get together then?" She slid out of the booth and headed for the door.

She glanced up in the mirror and saw that he sat in the booth with his head in his hands. She thought he might actually be crying. She stood and stared at the reflection for the longest time, trying to imagine what could possibly be tormenting him so. She turned and headed out to the street.

She had just crossed to the other side, so that she was standing on northwest corner of the *Chronicle* building when she heard him call her name. She didn't turn, but instead kept walking. He called her name again, this time with more urgency, as he stood in the middle of the street.

"It wasn't right, Thea," he said. "It wasn't right, and I did it anyway."

Thea started to walk back to him, wondering what he was rambling about. And in the same instant that she turned to face him, a car sped around the corner and struck him with such force, he was thrown fifteen feet down the block. As Thea stood in horror, the car sped away. There was no one else on the street.

After the shock had worn off to a dull ache, Thea knew she had to get to the bottom of whatever it was he had discovered. His death was no accident, and she worked for months to try to piece together what could have led to it. She poured through piles of documents, with Ted helping alongside, reviewing correspondence from Tom's office, and talking to everyone at the mayor's office who might have known something. She found nothing.

And then, six months after Tom died, a construction company that been awarded a public works contract to erect a public school in the city found itself embroiled in a legal battle when the school collapsed on a Tuesday morning, killing twenty-nine children and injuring hundreds of others. The same construction firm that had done the project had been awarded, just three days before Tom died, the most lucrative of all public projects in the Western Addition. The car that had run Tom down had been registered to a brick mason working for the same construction company.

Thea worked for weeks on the story, and when it broke, it was on the front page of the *Chronicle*. The follow-up stories, written by others as well as Thea, captured everyone's attention in the city for months. At the end of the investigation, which Thea pressed to conclusion, four people were indicted by a grand jury for obstruction of justice, conspiracy, and fraud. The mayor resigned under pressure from the board of supervisors.

No one was ever charged in Tom's accident.

Max Schuyler's decision to sell the bar seemed a fitting close to this chapter of Thea's life. He was sixty-five, and he was ready to go fishing in Florida, he said. A real estate developer had offered him a good price, and he decided to take it.

"More office space. Just what we need down here. Pretty soon there won't be any place to get a drink," Max muttered. "I'd better cash the check the day I get it, before they have time to reconsider," he smirked.

He was making light, but he had been tortured over the decision. This wasn't just his business, it had become his life. His friends were here, his social structure. His kids had long since grown and gone, and he'd never remarried after his wife died of cancer seven years ago. Thea couldn't figure out if he was convincing her or himself when he talked about how much he would enjoy his retirement. As she watched his face those last few weeks, she concluded he was trying to convince himself he'd made the right decision, and Thea and the other regulars did their part to help.

"Man, retirement. You lucky bastard," grimaced Pete Baker. "I'll probably die right at my desk, hunched over a typewriter."

"With a knife in your back, most likely," one of the writers fired back. "You know how mad a writer can get when he doesn't like the edits."

Thea did her part as well. She bought Max a fishing pole and hat. She told him he should take the proceeds from the sale of the bar to buy himself a fishing boat.

The last night at Schuyler's was an event to be remembered. Anyone who had ever appeared in the *Chronicle*'s city section was there, as were a handful of socialites and sports celebrities. Everyone had an "I remember when..." story of one sort or another that embarrassed Max, but it was obvious that he was touched by all the attention.

Thea put on a good face, but she could hardly come in here without thinking of Tom. She knew she had to be here tonight. Nan hadn't even bothered to ask her about it, the assumption was so clear that the two of them would be going. Thea hadn't looked in the mirror over the bar the last few times she had been in. The first time she came back in here after Tom's accident, when she looked up, the image of him waving at her from the front door was so clear, she was sure he was there. It frightened her, and she went back to the office before she even got her coat off. She just wasn't ready, she thought.

But tonight, it seemed fitting that she should say her good-byes. The mirror had most likely been sold, and it would be gone on to some other owner, new stories to observe and unravel. She heard a chorus of laughter as someone finished another toast and story to Max, and her eyes traveled up over the bar. The mirror was gone. She froze, staring at the empty hole in the wall. She assumed it had been sold, but the stark reality of it missing from that spot was overwhelming. The look on her face must have been obvious.

"Looks so empty, doesn't it?" Max said. "I never really paid much attention to it until it was gone."

"Did someone buy it?"

"Yeah... said he was giving it to a friend."

Thea's heart sunk. She sat silently and stared into the empty space, and all of the emotion from the last year poured out of every part of her being. She lay her head down on the bar and started to cry. She cried for Max. She cried for Tom. She cried for herself.

A hand touched her shoulder and she looked up. It was Max, who'd come around the bar.

"Come with me. I need to show you something."

She crawled down off the stool, turning her face away from the crowd, trying to hide her blotchy face and eyes, and followed Max into the back office. She realized in all of the time she had been coming here, she never knew there was a back office. She assumed there was, but she never even noticed the back door. She went through it now, following Max into a small room that had a large desk, a leather chair, and a library-type lamp. It was filled with boxes, stuff that Max wanted to keep, she assumed, and a few other pieces of random furniture. Max walked around behind the desk and pulled out a large, flat package, heavy, from the way Max was lifting it.

"I want you to have this."

Thea looked up, puzzled, but she instinctively knew what it was.

"What? You think you're the only person who watched what went on in this place? People used to say I had eyes in the back of my head. When I first opened this place in '06, kids used to try and come in and take stuff off the tables when they thought I couldn't see 'em. I always had another set of eyes." He smiled at her, gently. "I used to watch you waiting for him. As long as I live, I will never forget the look on your face when you saw him in the mirror."

Thea started to pull back the covering, and as she did, the tears came again.

"Max, where did it come from?"

"I had just started thinking about opening this place when the big quake struck in '06. There were a whole slew of homes and buildings that were destroyed in the fires afterwards, and before they razed them to rebuild, they paid people to clear the debris out. I had a buddy, knew I was thinking about opening a place, and he said, 'You know, there's probably stuff in those piles that's usable, a little burned, or scraped, but you never know.' So I went up with him to the job site he was working on, and started sifting through some of the rubble."

Thea sat, fascinated by his story. That this mirror had survived the earthquake and the fire seemed inconceivable to her. It also gave her a big breath of renewed hope.

"It had been on some sort of base, I think, because it had part of a frame around it, but it was all busted up, and the base was nowhere to be found. The glass in the mirror was all smashed up, but I figured that could be replaced easily enough, and it just seemed like the right size for what I was thinking. Paid the guy seventy-five cents for it."

Thea looked at it more closely as he was telling her the story and noticed that indeed it had been probably used vertically, instead of horizontally, the way Max had it over the bar, because there were two wooden pins in each side that had been sheared off. She figured that that had been where it attached to the base. Some kind of dressing mirror, probably. Now that she really studied it, she saw all the fine detail in the outer frame as well. The carvings were quite intricate, not ornate, but lovely. She never really noticed them above the bar.

"Anyway, I had the glass replaced, the guy told me it was real old, I should hang onto it. Been over the bar ever since." He stopped briefly, as if he was thinking back to when he first opened the place. He seemed to get a bit melancholy momentarily.

"Max, you have provided so many people with so many hours of enjoyment, so many memories. This place is a part of all of us. We may find a new watering hole, but there will never be another Schuyler's." She touched his hand lightly and said, "and now I have a part of it, too. It will stay with me forever."

She walked around the desk to embrace him, and as she did, she thought she could feel a slight shake in his shoulders. A riotous roar went up outside, and Max pulled back. He wiped his cheek with the back of his hand.

"I better get back out there before they destroy the place. I sold all the furniture to some guy over in Berkeley, and he's coming for it tomorrow. I suspect he'd be a little irritated if it's all busted up."

Thea and Max both laughed and made their way out of the office and back to the bar. But before she closed the door behind her, she took one last glance in the mirror and looked at her reflection.

Not a broken soul, she thought, *just a little bruised.*

She sees it all as some sort of problem to be solved. She doesn't know that I can tell her what she needs to know if she only looks and listens. I will not be valuable to her because she knows where I have been. I can only be valuable to her if she allows herself to really see the reflection. She rarely looks my way, unless it is to see the reflection of something else. She does not see herself. I do not know if it is because she thinks she already knows what is here or if she is afraid to really look. Of all those that have come before, she is the greatest mystery.

I think she has no soul.

Beth—2002

Beth was racing to make a 6:45 A.M. flight to Orange County. She knew it had been a bad idea to stay out at the beach last night, and the traffic had been worse than she'd thought it would be. She still had to find a place in the parking garage and get to the gate. It was a day trip, so no luggage, only her laptop bag and her purse, so she ought to get through security pretty handily. Still, it would be tight. There would be no upgrade today. Oh, well, if you have to sit in coach, she thought, a fifty-five-minute flight isn't so bad.

She sat, panting, in her seat from having run through the terminal because, of course, she was at Gate 90, the furthest one out, but she wasn't thinking about work. She was thinking about the mirror.

The "furniture doctor" that Jeff Hancock had recommended had done a beautiful job. The wood was restored to its natural cherry tone, and he had cleaned up a lot of the scratches and dings that it had accumulated over the years. Beth thought she might have a new base made and return it to its original dressing mirror stance, but the furniture doctor thought this was risky. The way the wood pins had been sheared off when the frame broke off weakened the sides, and he thought the whole thing might split open if they were removed or replaced. He also said he didn't think that new pins would be able to hold the weight of a frame.

So, Beth abandoned that plan and then thought briefly about hanging it vertically, the way it was originally intended, but the reflection of the ocean and the view up the beach was not nearly as spectacular. She'd keep it horizontal. Now that it looked better, she had grown quite attached to it. She could watch Drew coming back from his run, all the way up the beach until he appeared on the deck. She also could see some of their other neighbors, running, sunning, even gardening. She thought of it as her little window to the world out there.

She told Robert Allen that his mother was more lucid than he seemed to give her credit for. When Beth and Drew met with him to get the deed recorded, she mentioned that she had visited his mother.

"One of the interesting phenomena about Alzheimer's is the ability to call on past memory with great clarity. But I guarantee, if you had walked back in to see her fifteen minutes after leaving, she would not have had any idea who you were or what you had talked about."

"Well, she remembered the 1940s as if they were yesterday."

"She probably thought they were yesterday," he said, without ever looking up from his paperwork. "All the same, I'm glad you found what you wanted."

"Well, part of what I wanted. I know how Dorothea got the mirror and where it came from before that, but I still don't know how it got from England to San Francisco, and I'm still puzzling over a comment your mother made."

"Oh, what was that?"

"Something about two great loves coming in the mirror. You wouldn't know anything about that, would you?"

It was then that Drew interrupted.

"Please excuse my wife, Mr. Allen. She hasn't seemed to outgrow her desire to be Nancy Drew." Drew shot Beth a look that was obviously a plea to stop.

Robert Allen laughed.

"Actually, I think it's quite fascinating. Intellectual curiosity is a trait that's often overlooked, Mr. Graham," he said slowly. "In this day and age, everyone wants an answer right this second. They have no patience to investigate or explore." He glanced over at Beth, "I think it's fascinating. But unfortunately, I have no idea what my mother was talking about."

Beth looked at Drew as if to say, "see?" She felt somewhat vindicated.

"How about the name Jack Kennedy? Does that mean anything to you?"

"Besides it being the ex-president?"

"Besides that," she said with an embarrassed smile. "Someone your mother might have known, or Dorothea Renton?"

"Sorry, doesn't ring any bells."

Now, sitting on the plane, with her cold coffee and a bagel she'd brought in her bag, she wanted to know more.

Since they were still parked at the gate, she made a quick call on her cell phone. At this hour of the morning, she knew she would only get her voice mail, but that would be good enough.

The phone rang its customary four rings before cutting over to voice mail. Once she heard the tone, she started.

"Kim, it's me, Beth. I'm headed to Orange County for a meeting this morning, but I'll be back early, like

2:30 or something like that. You can check my itinerary. I'm coming back to the office, and I need to see you when I get in. I have more research for you."

Beth arrived back at the office around 3:45, and Kim was sitting at her desk waiting for her.

"So what's all the hubbub?" Kim asked.

"Okay, the mirror was made in 1881—"

"I thought we were done with this?"

"Me, too. But I changed my mind. Hear me out."

Kim plopped down in the visitor's chair in Beth's office.

"You know, these chairs are so uncomfortable. Not very inviting."

"Dan and Bill picked them solely for that reason. They didn't want people loafing around in other people's offices, bullshitting around. They figured if the chairs were really uncomfortable, it would cut the kitsching down to a minimum and they'd get more billable hours out of everyone."

"You're kidding me."

"Nope. Okay, let me continue—your ass will fall asleep in that chair in about two minutes. The mirror is made in 1881 in England, probably London, by someone at William Morris, initials TES. Somehow it ends up in San Francisco in 1906. How does it get there?"

"Whoever bought it moves to San Francisco from London?"

"Okay, that's one possible theory. Fast forward. Dorothea Renton gets hold of it in 1945, after it being in the bar since 1906. It ends up in her beach house when I get there in 2002."

"Yeah, so?"

"So, where was the mirror in the missing years?"

"Oh, no. No more research. Max Schuyler's great grandson turned out to be a little twisted. I'm done."

"No more living research. The periods of time we need to know about are historical. We're going to have to piece it together without people. This is real research."

"I might have to go somewhere. You know, to really research it right. Like London," Kim managed to say with a serious straight face.

"Nice try. Let's see what we can accomplish at San Francisco Main before we start reserving rooms at Claridge's, shall we?"

"You're really becoming a grouch."

"Hey, Kim?" Beth called after her, watching her massage her butt. She was pretty sure it had fallen asleep in that chair. She smiled slightly. "You think we should ask Mr. Three Last Names to do some grunt work on this?"

"He'll want a client number. He does nothing because he's a nice guy."

"Okay, let's hold that thought. We might need to play that card later. In the meantime, you and I are going 'off site' tomorrow to work on a project. I'll meet you at San Francisco Main at nine in the morning. Okay?"

"Okay. You're the boss."

"Let's start with English period furniture." They both sat huddled around the terminal at the main library, familiarizing themselves with the search functionality and the map of the library. Beth hadn't been in here since it had been renovated, so she didn't know her way around all that well. The reference listing came up and continued for several pages. The stark reality of this being a long process started to set in.

"Kim, we're going to need to divide and conquer. I'll keep working on this. You start researching 1906. See if you can get a list or something of all the buildings that were damaged or lost in the earthquake."

Kim raised her eyebrows quizzically.

"And I would be asking for that because . . . ?"

"Because we think that most of the furniture in the bar was reclaimed from earthquake damaged buildings at very low cost. So maybe we can figure out where it came from."

Kim rolled her eyes, already understanding that the task that lay before her was huge. But she had to admit, she was intrigued.

Leaving Beth to sort through English period furniture, Kim went in search of the reference librarian. When in doubt, enlist the help of a professional.

The reference librarian did not seem daunted by the task at all. In fact, the older woman seemed thrilled with some sort of mission.

"Let's start with public records. We can probably find parcel maps that would show buildings lost or damaged."

In fact, they did find maps that showed the areas that were damaged or completely destroyed. In all, 28,000 structures were lost. The librarian took her into an archive room to begin looking through microfiche.

"We're in the process of putting most of this on CDs, but we're starting with the most recent and working our way backward. Anything before about 1930 is still on the fiche."

The librarian was able to find parcel maps, which showed the areas of damage, and then in a stroke of total, dumb luck, Kim came across a listing of "displaced persons" and their addresses. Most of it was commercial, but in all likelihood, a mirror like that would have been residential, so now the list of addresses reduced down to about one third the original number. Progress.

While the displaced persons listing was printing, at fifteen cents per page, she sat thinking about how much she was enjoying this. It was a cross between detective work and grunt work, but she had to admit the satisfaction of finding a good tidbit and then connecting it to something else was rewarding. She remembered Beth saying she would help her with her case for being promoted to research assistant. When Beth had mentioned it, Kim was somewhat nonplussed. Why would she want to sit in a cubicle all day and run around the web? But now that she was getting into it, she began to get her hopes up about moving up. She was jolted out of her daydream by Beth's voice.

"Good God, what are you printing?" The printer stack had fallen over and was spilling onto the floor. Already forty-one pages had spewed out, and there was more coming.

"Addresses of displaced persons from the 1906 quake. Hopefully you are going to tell me exactly which page we will need."

"Not exactly," Beth grimaced. "Not yet, anyway."

"So what do you have to report?"

"William Morris was quite the prolific designer in the midnineteenth century. He designed buildings, furniture, all kinds of stuff. He had hundreds of apprentices, but only a handful that worked on commissioned pieces."

"Please tell me you have more than that," Kim began to see her research career being extremely brief.

Beth's face broke into a grin that gave her good fortune away.

"In 1882, he expanded his reach to the new territory of Australia. He took one of his best artisans and opened a shop in Sydney. He stayed for about six months and left the apprentice behind to grow the business."

"I'm lost. Does this have something to do with the mirror? Was it made in Australia?"

"I don't think so. Remember, it was made for the queen, so it must have been made in London."

"So why do we care about him going to Australia?"

"Because the artisan that ran the business in Sydney was Thomas Edward Smyth—T-E-S." She paused to see if Kim could connect the dots.

"The initials under the William Morris signature on the mirror," Kim said in the next breath. "I hate to burst your bubble, but what if there's another T-E-S?"

Simultaneously, Beth and Kim looked at the stack of paper falling from the printer. Beth started picking up the pages and scanning them quickly. Ah, what luck, they were in alphabetical order. She searched the list for Smyth. There were two.

Beth glanced at her watch.

"Oh, God. I'm supposed to be on a conference call with Dan . . . five minutes ago."

"Go. I'll be here. Come back when you're done." Kim knew what she needed to do next.

She looked at the two Smyths. Thank God he spelled it with a "y." There were hundreds that spelled it with an "i." A. M. Smyth, an address up near USF, according to the parcel maps, and a J. Smyth on Nob Hill. The address on Nob Hill, however, was listed as vacant. *Not likely to have any furniture if it was vacant,* thought Kim. The other address, for A. M. Smyth was listed as a women's rooming house. *That sounds promising*, she thought. *Young women and mirrors seemed like a good combination.*

Kim got out her cell phone and then remembered where she was. She grabbed the printout with the two Smyth names on it, pitched the rest in the recycling bin and made her way outside. When she got to the sidewalk, she waved at Beth, who was standing on the far corner with her phone in her ear. She was saying nothing, but signaling to Kim the universal sign for "drowning" as she raised her hand and moved her thumb and the rest of her hand open and closed. Kim gave her a nod and then proceeded to make her call.

She was on the phone for quite a while, longer than it took Beth to finish her conference call.

Beth approached her.

"You'd think he invented the term 'business process reengineering' the way he—"

Kim held up her hand, and Beth noticed Kim was still on the phone.

"Oh, sorry," Beth whispered.

Kim continued her conversation with whoever was on the other end of the line.

"If I were to come up there in person, could someone release the information to me?"

Beth watched her face as she listened to the person on the other end of the line.

"Great. I'll ask for Abby at the Alumni Affairs Office." She hung up the phone and motioned to Beth. "C'mon, our off-site is moving to another location."

They drove up California Avenue to Masonic and then cut over into the neighborhood that housed USF.

Once a Catholic Jesuit School, in 1968 it had purchased the remaining land and buildings that had once been the San Francisco College for Women. Any records of female students back to the early 1900s would have come from there. The woman at the alumni office wasn't very encouraging, but she told Kim to come on up and see for herself.

When they arrived, Kim approached the desk.

"Hi, I called earlier. I'm looking for Abby?"

"That would be me." A small young woman, probably a student, came out from behind a desk and put out her hand. "Abby Nelson. Nice to meet you."

Kim extended her hand as well.

"Hi, I'm Kim Baxter and this is my friend Beth Graham. We are trying to find out some information about a female student that would have attended here in the early 1900s. Maybe 1903, '04, '06?"

"Well, she would not have attended USF."

Kim and Beth's faces both dropped.

"USF didn't admit women then, but the San Francisco College for Women did. USF 'acquired' what was left of it. Actually the name changed to Lone Mountain College in the sixties, so we might have some records. Do you have a name?"

"Yes, Smyth, initials A.M."

She turned to her desk and punched a whole series of keys on her keyboard.

"Nothing so far." She continued to punch the keyboard. "Wait. Here's something. Smyth, Anne-Margaret, 1906. Let me print this out for you."

Beth and Kim waited for what seemed an agonizingly long time until the woman handed them the printout.

Kim began to read aloud.

"Anne-Margaret Smyth, age twenty-two. Hometown, Sydney, Australia, graduate student in literature. Degree conferred 1905, advanced degree coursework completed 1906. San Francisco College for Women. Born 1884, deceased 1945 in Sydney, Australia."

"Deceased 1945? She wasn't in the building when it burned," said Beth quietly.

"But the mirror must have been."

They sat on the steps in front of the alumni office, sipping their coffee from across the street, pleased with their work.

Beth retraced the mirror's steps as she understood them. "Thomas Smyth makes the mirror in 1881 for Queen Victoria, who decides she doesn't like it for whatever reason, so he keeps it. He goes to Sydney to start a William Morris outpost, marries someone, they have a child. She comes to San Francisco to school, the mirror gets buried in the earthquake, and she for some reason, doesn't. Max Schuyler buys it for the bar, gives it to Dorothea Renton."

Kim was looking pretty pleased with herself.

"Hey, we're pretty good at this stuff, huh?"

"You are good," Beth smiled back. "Now if you can find out how Jack Kennedy fits in here, you will be officially classified as great."

"You never give up, do you?"

"Not unless I am absolutely forced to."

It has taken her a long time to get here, but she has finally arrived. She is comfortable in her own skin, with her own demons. She has learned to love the solitude, the aloneness of being alone. She stares blankly for hours and then is lost in her own world for days. I think this must be the process of creation, to be completely pulled under by your own imagination. And when she lifts her eyes, her soul is open for a moment, as if she is taking in a big gulp of life before going under again. The ocean restores her, speaks to her in a way that is a foreign language to most. I do not know what the ocean tells her.

That is between her and the ocean.

Dorothea—1960

"Nan, I know you are trying to be helpful, but you are really trying my patience."

"Thea, all I am saying is that your buying this place on your own is quite an undertaking."

"Translation—you think it will end in disaster."

"Well, that's a little extreme. Houses are a lot of work, a lot of upkeep. Do you think you can do it on your own?"

"Well, I guess I'll just have to find myself a really good handyman. Maybe he'll be willing to trade sex for fix-its."

"Oh, that's a good plan."

"Look, Nan. I made a lot of money on my last book and at the ripe old age of forty-two, it's not likely that I will find a husband who will be buying me a house. Even if I were to find a husband, he'd already have a house. I want this to be my house. All on my own. I can afford it, and I want it. Stop trying to rain on my parade."

"It's so secluded out here. Do you think you'll be safe?"

"That's why I like it. I can write in peace, and no one will bother me or know where I am or what I'm doing. Besides, if I get murdered, no one will find me for days and I can be on the front page of the *Chronicle*, just like I always wanted."

"I'm sure Pete Baker just turned over in his grave

when he heard you say that."

"RIP, my friend, you cranky old bastard."

They both laughed as they headed to the car.

Thea reached out and grabbed Nan's arm.

"Hey, before we head back to the city, come take a walk with me. Maybe then you will understand why I have to buy this place."

They walked around the side of the house towards the ocean. It was a good distance from the porch to the ocean but it was a gentle decline to the sea. Once they got to the water line, they walked north. There were very few homes, only a few scattered here and there. Dorothea's had been built in the fifties sometime, just ahead of the change in the building regulations. It was much tougher to get a permit to build now, so here serenity was pretty much guaranteed, at least for a while.

The sun was beginning to sink on the horizon, and there had been just enough high cloud cover to produce a breathtaking sunset. The indigo faded to pink, which faded to a pale orange and stretched all the way back toward Mt. Tamalpais.

"Boy, I could get used to that view every night," Nan said, in a hushed tone. They had stopped walking and were sitting in the sand, watching the sky change colors.

"Well, I'm sure it will be shrouded in fog from May to September, but it's nice now."

"So, you'll write in Hawaii from May to September."

"Good idea."

"Let's head back. I've got a dinner tonight, and I have to pick the boys up and get them fed first," Nan motioned for the house.

They walked back the way the had come, and when they reached the house Nan was out of breath.

"Man, the walk back is a killer. It doesn't seem like that much of a slope going out."

"It's deceiving. Think what great-looking legs I'll have in six months if I do that every day."

"Will make bagging that handyman a lot easier." They giggled as they brushed the sand off their feet, put on their shoes, and headed for the car.

"Back to the city Jeeves," said Thea.

"Yes, Miss Renton," Nan replied.

The solitude at the ocean was something that Thea would never grow tired of. She was always alone, but she was never lonely. She was passing from her first season there, fall, into winter, and the newness of every day was thrilling to her. The light changed dramatically as the days grew shorter and the temperature dropped. The beach had also grown empty, the last remnants of fall tourists all but gone. Occasionally she'd see a mother with a young child down on the sand, too young for school, taking it all in. *What must a two-year-old think of all this?* she thought to herself one morning. Thea didn't recall seeing the ocean until some time in her teenage years, and even then she had been awed by it. *A two-year-old probably doesn't fathom the vastness of it*, she thought, as she watched him intent on digging up sand, grain by grain.

Winter was quickly becoming her favorite season, although she had said that about the fall as well. She suspected she might feel the same about the spring. But there was something about the clear, crispness of January and the absolute desolateness of the beach that sang to her. People had seen whales out here on occasion, as they made their way down to Baja California to breed, and although she had purchased a set of binoculars in the off-chance she might actually see one, she hadn't used them so far. Still, she liked the idea of them, and she kept them on her mantle in the event she needed them to spot a wayward mammal.

Thea noticed an intense stillness, a silence about the beach that she couldn't quite describe. The ocean swell was much lower, unless it was stormy, and the sound of the waves breaking was soft and muted. She would lie awake in the morning in her bed and close her eyes and try to find a pattern in the waves, but there was none. Even though waves theoretically broke in sets, the pattern in the winter was more erratic. Still, the surfers that bobbed about out there would wait, hopeful, freezing in their dark black suits.

She was furnishing the place one piece at a time. When she had decided to live out here full time, she didn't move any furniture from her apartment in the city. She really wanted to start over. She moved only her four-poster bed, her writing desk, and a big, overstuffed chaise chair, which was the only thing to sit on in her living room. She didn't have guests. When Nan came out, which wasn't often, they sat on the deck or at her kitchen counter, which had two high stools, left by the previous owner.

But the centerpiece of the room was the mirror. She was unable to hang it at first; the emotional disruption it caused her when she moved it was a surprise to her. It had been hanging in the same spot in her apartment since Max had given it to her, and she really hadn't given it much thought in the fifteen years she'd had it there. A quick glance to check her hair, tie a scarf, never really looking at it very deeply. Her image in the mirror wasn't something she stared at.

But as it was dislodged from its spot in her apartment, so were all the old feelings and memories, hitting Thea so hard, it was as if she was reliving them. She kept it on the floor of her bedroom at the beach house until she thought she could hang it. But she did think about the right spot, almost daily. She toyed with the idea of hanging it vertically, using it as a dressing mirror in her bedroom, but thought better of it. I don't need to see myself or what I'm wearing. No, the spot would have to be one that reflected something else. The mirror had always been a symbol to her, a window to something else, someone else. She would not hang the mirror until the place to hang it was so obvious to her that she would be disappointed she hadn't discovered it earlier.

So one afternoon in December, she opened her eyes sleepily after dozing off in her overstuffed chair, book still opened to the page she had left, and noticed that the sunset had cast a lovely palette of color along her living room wall. She instinctively walked to her bedroom, picked up the mirror from the floor, and returned to the living room and leaned the mirror against the wall. She was awestruck by the reflection. It was if the sunset had entered the room and reflected all of the color, the vibrancy, the depth of the horizon into her living room.

She rooted through her kitchen drawer until she found a hammer and two picture hanger attachments. She carefully measured to the midpoint of the wall and chose a height at just above eye level. Given the weight of the mirror, she knew she needed to find a wall stud for at least one of the hanger attachments. She began tapping with her knuckle, listening for a deeper-sounding tone. When she located it, she realized she would have to adjust the location just slightly.

Once she had it hung, she turned back to her chair, keeping her eyes closed while she settled into her usual half-sitting, half-sleeping position. She knew the angle of the mirror would need to be perfect from this position.

She slowly opened her eyes and caught her breath. She could see the entire horizon, still ablaze with color. She could see the beach line northward, probably two miles or so. Eventually, it faded into the horizon, and the line between ocean and sky became one. She sighed and discovered for the first time in fifteen years that the image in this mirror was the image it was meant to see. All the time she had the mirror in her apartment, she never gave it more than a glance, never letting the reflection become part of her. Sitting here, staring at the mirror now, she let go of all of the old sorrow and allowed the reflection inside.

"You know, that wall is just way too big for that mirror," Nan announced, as she entered the room. "If you're going to leave it there, you should put a few other pieces around it."

"I am leaving it there, and I don't want 'other pieces' to detract from it."

"Detract from it? That would be impossible."

"Look, that mirror means a lot to me, and you know it. Why do you feel the necessity to be so cruel?" Thea snapped back.

"I know it means a lot to you. I'm just suggesting you might be able to enhance it a bit. It's so dark for this room. Maybe we should paint it."

"Paint it? It's nineteenth-century cherry wood. We don't paint it."

"What about antiquing it? You know, where you sort of brush the stuff on and off and the wood still shows through, but it looks like it's been washed in color," Nan implored.

"No," Thea replied briskly.

"Just hear me out. Then you can piss on my idea."

"That sounds promising . . . the pissing on your idea part."

"I know you told me you didn't want my help with this place, and I graciously accepted that. But I have some great ideas for this room, you know, overstuffed furniture, light colors, maybe some green, some rose. C'mon, Thea, you know you have no eye for this stuff. Let me do it. It would be fun. You can have ultimate authority."

Thea laughed out loud.

"No I can't. Every time I say no, you convince me how wrong I am, and you get what you want. That's how our relationship works."

"Well, I told you not to buy this place, and you did anyway. So you got your way on that one."

"Let's see. That would be Thea 1 and Nan 419, for those of you keeping score at home."

"Please, Thea. Please, please, please." Nan held her hands together and pouted like a four-year-old asking for dessert.

"You might just be one of the most pathetic women I know, Nan."

"Sad but true. I live vicariously through you and your characters. I'll be Marcy from *The Dark Alley*."

"You are Marcy from *The Dark Alley*."

"I knew it! You lied to me about that."

"I didn't want to hurt your feelings. She was pretty shallow."

"Yes, but she saved her friend from depression and suicide."

"Only because every time she thought about killing herself, she realized her life wasn't nearly as bad as Marcy's."

"Details. Besides, these are fictional characters. I know Marcy was actually a blend of people. The good decorating taste was me; the shallow part was someone else."

Thea laughed.

"Your ability to justify knows no bounds. You know that, right?"

"One of my many fine qualities," Nan replied with a smile. "You haven't said no yet."

"If I say yes, will you stop setting me up on blind dates with friends of Bill?"

Nan thought for a moment.

"That's not a fair request. What if I find you the perfect mate?"

Thea rolled here eyes. The chances that Nan would find her the perfect mate were zero. She always picked men exactly like her husband, whom Thea couldn't stand.

"Decorating or matchmaking, you pick."

"Well, it pains me, but I'll go with decorating. I suspect I will never be successful at matchmaking because you have a bad attitude."

"Wait until you see my attitude about decorating."

Thea had to admit it; when Nan was finished, it

looked beautiful. It was exactly what she had pictured when she described to Nan what she wanted. She couldn't describe the colors or the textures, but she described in vivid detail what she wanted to feel like when she was in the room: "Serene, you know, peaceful, relaxed, quiet. I want to feel like I'm in my own refuge, even though I live here."

Nan had been amazingly quiet during those early days, Thea just assumed she wasn't listening, but she had been. To every word.

She made an ocean oasis out of the front room. Everything that Thea had described about bringing the outdoors in was done. Nan replaced the sliding doors with French doors that opened out onto the deck, so the deck became an extension of the living area. She painted the walls a soft sage green, and in addition to Thea's favorite overstuffed chaise, which was re-covered, she added an antiqued green table and two more side chairs. And after all the arguing, Thea had to admit, the mirror looked magnificent.

Just as Nan had described, the pale green was brushed on and then wiped off, leaving streaks where the cherry wood peeked through. Nan had some of the scratches filled, and the corner where Max had said that the wood was scarred from fire was hidden beneath the pale green brush strokes. She chose some other pieces to surround it on the wall that complemented it beautifully. The mirror was still the star of the wall, but the surrounding pieces brought your eyes and attention back to the mirror.

Nan found two smaller mirrors, rectangular shaped, but in oval white-washed frames that she hung to either side. She installed a high shelf above the mirror where she placed a shadow box with sand dollars and shells. On the other end of the shelf, she had a photo of a group of them in front of the Schuyler's sign. Thea thought it might have been taken the last night that Schuyler's was open, but she didn't really remember it. The frame was antiqued in the same green as the mirror.

"It's beautiful, Nan," Thea said quietly. She was quite taken aback by the whole room, once she stood to look at it.

"You thought I wasn't listening, didn't you."

Thea smiled.

"I was wrong." She plopped down in her favorite chaise and sighed a long, deep sigh. "I feel exactly the way I want to feel in this room."

Nan beamed. For the first time in her adult life, she felt accomplished.

"Thank you for letting me do this."

Thea took her hand.

"There are so many things that I love about you, Nan. I love that you wanted to get married to a doctor, so you did. I love that you wanted to have three sons, so you did. I love that you wanted to learn to make Chicken Cordon Bleu, so you went to cooking school in Paris. I love that despite your feelings about my buying this place, you wanted to help me make it a home, so you did."

She paused and looked out to the ocean. "I used to always tell people that you and I were friends because you were all the things I wasn't." Thea turned back and looked beyond Nan and into the mirror on the opposite wall. "But we're pretty similar creatures, you and I. Even though what we want couldn't be more different, we both have a singular focus about getting it. I create feelings with words, you create feelings with space."

Nan turned to look in the mirror.

"Do you ever see his face?"

"I used to. Now I just see mine. And whatever that view has to share with me."

The morning had been dreary, and Thea was having trouble staying focused on her writing. She kept reminding herself of Virginia Woolf's theory. You only need to write 250 words in a day. As long as they are the best 250 words you are capable of. Of course, Virginia Woolf suffered from mental illness and committed suicide, so maybe she wasn't the best person from whom to be taking advice.

As she stared down at the pages, she realized she hadn't even mastered 250 words today, let alone her best 250 words. Some days, it just didn't come as easily as others. Today was one of those days. Maybe a different chair. She left her pen and pages behind and fell into her chaise.

It had stopped raining, and the sun was beginning to pop through. It looked like the storm was clearing and the afternoon might be promising. She glanced in the mirror and saw a few brave souls out walking the beach, probably looking for treasures. Storms brought shells, driftwood, and occasionally some sea glass. She had taken to using the mirror to allow her the ability to voyeur the activity on the beach. It seemed lazy to sit and watch it all unfold without actually taking part, but it also allowed her the time to insert herself in the image, to find herself in the middle of a story.

What kind of guy walks alone on the beach at the same time every day? This was her latest question.

She noticed him several weeks ago, and then continued to notice him every day at exactly the same time, even on the days when it rained. She had even gone so far as to take her whale-watching binoculars out of their case on the shelf to see if she knew him. She didn't. He wasn't a resident, at least not a permanent resident; Thea knew all of those by now. But still he came, every day, and walked the same stretch of beach. She could see him coming, far in the distance. The mirror always carried his reflection for a long time before Thea could actually make him out. She watched him walk, methodically, purposefully.

Since the skies were clearing, she opened her doors, and the sound caught his attention. He stopped and looked her way briefly, then continued on. She removed the cover from one of her deck chairs and watched the water fall off the cover to the deck below. It dripped through the wood planks and all the way to the sand underneath. She sat and stared at the beach and lost track of time, until suddenly he appeared in her view. He had a stick in his hand that he was throwing and then picking up as he reached it. She was more than a little curious, so she grabbed her beach shoes, soaking wet from having been left on the deck, and headed down to the sand. Their paths intersected just as she reached the water line.

"Hello," she said.

"Hello," he replied, without looking at her.

"I've seen you out here every day for the last few weeks. Are you staying out here?" she realized she was being nosy.

"Uh-huh. For a few months, I'm staying at the Porters' house while they are gone. Do you know it?"

"Sure. Where are the Porters?"

She had met them shortly after she moved in last September, but it suddenly occurred to her she hadn't seen them since before Christmas.

"Traveling for a few months—somewhere warmer, I suspect." He offered her a slight smile as he dug his hands deeper into his pockets. "You a year-rounder out here?"

"So far, I am. I just bought the place in September, so I don't really qualify for year-rounder status yet, but that's the idea." She thrust her hand out and introduced herself, "I'm Thea Renton. I live—"

"Oh, the writer. Sam told me about you. You live right up there." He said, pointing to her house.

"Yes. Sam told you about me?"

"He gave me the names and phone numbers of a few neighbors. In case I wanted to throw a dinner party," he smiled sarcastically.

"Yes, you look like quite the entertainer," she replied, looking down and moving the sand around with her foot. The rain had packed it down to wet cement, so pushing it around with her foot was requiring some effort. She wondered if he could tell how much she was laboring to look perfectly natural.

"Looks can be deceiving. I'm actually quite handy with a corkscrew. Would have to have the rest catered, though."

Thea smiled and looked back at him. He was younger than Thea, she thought, thirty-five maybe. He was tall, probably six feet two or three inches, dark brown hair, and he had green eyes. Very green. He had a nice build, more than nice, actually. In fact, Thea found herself a little distracted. She looked down at his hands, which came out of his pockets when she introduced herself. Hands were very important to Thea. Hands said everything. Some women liked eyes, some liked thighs, some liked chest and shoulders; Thea liked hands. She loved long, thin fingers, perfectly shaped fingernails. And they had to be strong.

She tried to imagine what he did for a living. He was out here in the middle of the week, so whatever it was, it didn't have regular hours. He didn't strike her as Bohemian enough to be an artist or a writer. And his hands definitely didn't suggest any kind of manual labor. When he shook her hand, it was smooth on the underside.

"I'm a professor at Princeton University," he said, suddenly, as though he knew instinctively what she was thinking. "Philosophy," he said. "I'm taking the winter term off, ostensibly to do research, but I haven't done a thing since I've been out here." He laughed slightly. "Thank God for tenure. I don't think they can sack me if I come back for spring term not published."

"Philosophy. And what is it that you claim to be researching out here?" she inquired with a note of skepticism.

"I'm not really researching anything here. I just find the ocean a nice place to work. I'm actually researching the impact of the great political thinkers on modern day political systems." He laughed quickly. "Now, there's a real page turner, huh?"

Thea laughed.

"I took one philosophy course in college, and even then only because it was required. I didn't think much of it." Thea thought to herself, *Maybe I'd have liked it more if you had been teaching it.*

"Well, you either love it or hate it. Me, I loved the way it made me think about other things. Philosophy is a great reflection of the human soul. Guess I was trying to find mine."

A flock of seagulls suddenly took flight from about fifteen yards away. Their white underbellies against the steel-gray sky with the sun's reflection on them were spectacular.

"Wow. Look at that. Think they got spooked by something?" Thea asked as she held her hand up to her eyes to shield them from the sun.

"Yeah, my talking philosophy. Tends to have that effect on people."

Thea laughed.

"A philosopher with a sense of humor. Now, that has to be quite a rarity."

He glanced down at his watch.

"I'm sorry, I've got to get going. It was nice to meet you, Thea."

He turned back up toward the Porter house and began to jog away. *Probably riding off to meet some gorgeous woman,* Thea thought sadly.

"You didn't tell me your name," Thea called after him.

He smirked as though he was in some sort of pain.

"It's Jack. Jack Kennedy. No relation to the guy soon to be in the White House."

Thea smiled back at him, and then watched him walk up the beach, until he was no longer in sight.

"See you later, Jack Kennedy," and she headed for her house.

She found herself starting to glance in the mirror just

after three every day. By 3:30 if he hadn't appeared she started to wonder. But inevitably, she would see him walking down the beach. She could make out his outline from a long ways by now. She knew his build, his gait, and he was always throwing a stick to an imagined dog.

But his routine changed slightly. Now, as he approached her house, he would cut up into the sand and head for her deck. When he did, she'd run into the house, pull back her hair, put on a little lipstick. Then she'd open the doors onto the deck, her sign that she was home and expecting company. Moments later, he would be standing on her deck, stick and imagined dog left on the sand below.

It was a mutually beneficial relationship. She helped him think about his research, ask questions. He got to know her characters and helped her with her book.

"She would never say that, Thea," he would offer when she got stuck on a character's motivation. "She is too into herself to care about what he thinks."

So, they served as reciprocal muses for the next several weeks, getting to know each other better, sharing a bottle of wine now and then to "stimulate creativity," and then, suddenly, one day as the rain was pelting the outside deck, he leaned over and kissed her, tentatively at first, but when she responded, his tongue explored further.

They met most every afternoon. They talked, they wrote, they slept, they made love, and without fail, they watched the sunset every day. Thea knew it was fleeting. She knew it would end in April. He would go back to Princeton, and she would go back to the life she had before. But despite that, both of them knowing how this book would end, they didn't think about it. They enjoyed the moments they had, and knew that they would enjoy them for as long as they lasted. Despite the temporary nature of their relationship, Thea had fallen for him, but she knew he could never be hers. She was only borrowing him and borrowing time.

Glimpses of spring began to show themselves; trees in the lane behind her house down Dune Road began to bud, and the rose bushes began to leaf out from their winter twig appearance. Despite her usual enthusiasm for a change of season, Thea knew that spring meant Jack's return to Princeton, the finishing of her book, and the onset of early tourists.

She sat on her chaise and watched his reflection while he packed the few belongings he had brought over to her place.

"Thea, there's something I want to ask you," he said, with his back to her.

She bolted upright. Although the idea of him staying had crossed her mind, they had never discussed it. In fact, she didn't really know how he felt about her at all. She had purposefully avoided those conversations because she didn't want him to feel like she was looking to reel him in. She was self-conscious enough about being a few years older than he was, and she didn't need him thinking she was some desperate older woman looking to get married and have a child while she still could. She also had to admit to herself that although she had thought about what life would be like with him, she wasn't interested in marrying him.

The three months they had spent together were incredible, and Thea thought it was probably solely due to both of them knowing it had no future. They were consumed only by what happened on any given day. It was actually quite liberating to know that you didn't really have to think about the future consequences of anything you did. There was no future to worry about.

She also realized that having reached middle age, she was settled into her life like an old comfortable shoe. She liked the solitude of it. She had friends when she needed them, but she had always been a bit of a loner, although she would never have described herself that way. She didn't want a full-time commitment. She wanted what she had. She didn't really need him to complete her.

He looked down at her hands as he took them in his.

"The Porters have asked me if I want the place again next winter. I've given it some thought, but I think definitely not."

Her heart sunk just a little.

"Well, you know, you probably want to try a different spot next year. Different surroundings might be a good motivator. And I'm sure they'll have no trouble renting it."

"I was thinking about a different spot—maybe Italy?"

"Italy's good. You could research Roman philosophers." She paused and thought briefly. "Are there any?"

"Mostly Greek."

"Oh, well, Greece is nice too."

"Yeah, I thought about Greece, but the food is bad there."

"So what did you decide?"

"Well, I definitely need to be someplace where I can work, be motivated, inspired."

"Uh-huh."

"And I just keep coming back to the same place," he looked directly into her eyes, "right here with you." He paused and then said, "I'm not in a position to make any kind of commitment, Thea. So, if you don't want this, then you just have to say so. It would be a pretty unconventional arrangement."

She put her arms around him and whispered into his ear.

"When God wants to punish you, he answers your prayers."

"That's pretty pessimistic," he said, pulling away to see her face.

She threw her head back and laughed.

"I didn't make it up. Some tormented woman writer who ultimately killed herself did." She laughed a little. "But you have to admit, there is definitely a thread of truth to it."

She stared at herself in the mirror and decided that maybe for the first time in her adult life, she was truly and absolutely content.

And so they settled into a comfortable routine. He arrived every year, just after New Year's, and she settled in to writing the moment he arrived. They had no contact with each other during the rest of the year. He could have been married with three kids in New Jersey, for all she knew. But she didn't think so. He never called anyone in Princeton the entire time he stayed with her in California, and if he harbored any guilt about his life there, she never saw it or felt it.

They lived each day one at a time and enjoyed the time they had together for as long as it lasted, until spring came and he returned to teaching. She used the spring to edit out her book; she carefully timed her book tours for the summer, when all the tourists descended on Stinson Beach, and in the fall, when the beach had returned to its slow, easy pace, she started to think about her next book.

She wrote sixteen books in twenty years, not all best-sellers, but each reflected her state of mind that winter, some darker than others. Altogether, Jack Kennedy and Dorothea Renton spent twenty-three winters together. He died at the age of fifty-eight after a brief illness. Princeton University contacted her when the dean found some of Jack's mail in his personal effects with her address. It was forwarded with a copy of his obituary from the Princeton paper.

She never knew how he spent his last days, and she didn't think about it much. She preferred to remember just one thing about him: his reflection in the mirror when he came bounding up the back steps to her deck, dropping the stick and the imagined dog at the bottom. Until she drew her last breath, she knew it would be burned in her mind forever.

I would like to say that her reflection is peaceful, but I think she knows very little peace. She seems never to be at rest, although she often seems content. She is driven by some internal expectation of her own, and I have concluded that she has known very little disappointment. There are no emotional scars that I can see, no real damage to deepen her spirit. Even when she has solved the riddles, she is still searching.

Will she know it when she finds it? I wonder.

Beth—2002

"Are you trying to channel Dorothea Renton back so we can ask her about the heating valves in the attic?"

Beth had decided to start reading Dorothea Renton's books just to see if she could learn anything more about her. Now that Kim was doing "real" research, as she called it, she couldn't send her on any more errands for the mirror. She decided that she had learned enough to satisfy her curiosity. So she'd never know who Jack Kennedy was. She wasn't entirely sure there was one.

Beth closed her eyes and held her hand to her forehead.

"Sorry, Dorothea says you'll need to call a heating and plumbing guy."

"What is that, number three?"

"It's actually four. There's a distinct difference in this one from the other three. Almost seems like a different writer. But, then again, this one was written in 1961, so it could have been drug-induced."

"Maybe you can write a retrospective about her when you've finished all nineteen."

"Twenty. But she didn't finish the last one."

Beth flipped through the book, assessing the remaining length. She flipped to the last page, the acknowledgments. She remembered reading in another book somewhere that the acknowledgment page should always be read last, because it is the only place in the book where you hear the author's true voice. Read it too soon, and your ability to be inside the characters is somewhat diminished. Good rule, she thought, but she now ignored it.

This book would not have been possible without the loving and gentle hand of my editor, Julie Clarke. I couldn't be more blessed to have her in my corner. My agent and dear friend, Nan Allen, thank you a hundred times over for making my public life as painless as possible and for insuring all of my dealings with big, bad publishing are completely transparent.

And to J.K., my muse, my friend, my true partner in all things spiritual, physical, and emotional. You have been God's greatest gift to me, and I will treasure you always.

Beth sat bolt upright. J.K. Jack Kennedy? She stood up and walked to the mirror, with Drew's eyes upon her. She touched the wood softly and closed her eyes. When she reopened them, Drew was standing behind her, staring at their reflection and the reflection beyond them up the beach.